MURDER ON A LONELY BOG

A Cranberry Country Mystery

by

Edward Lodi

ROCK VILLAGE
PUBLISHING

Middleborough, Massachusetts

FIRST PRINTING

Murder on a Lonely Bog
Copyright © 2014 by Edward Lodi

Cover Photo: "A Lonely Bog"
Copyright © 2014 by Yolanda Lodi

Typography and cover design by Senco Printing, Inc.

ISBN 978-1-934400-35-7

Rock Village Publishing
41 Walnut Street
Middleborough MA 02346

(508) 946-4738

rockvillage@verizon.net

CONTENTS

MURDER ON A LONELY BOG

PROLOGUE:
Spring Peepers

He returned with the wheelbarrow to the gap in the stone wall where, a half hour earlier, he had left her body hidden in the shadows. The moon slid from behind thinning clouds to shine full upon her. Lying there exposed—her head propped against the base of the wall, her face smooth and pale against lichen-encrusted boulders, her angular features softened by moonglow—Amanda looked more lovely than ever, like a mannequin displayed to full advantage in a shop window. The bruise on her cheek might have passed for a beauty mark, the gash on her forehead for a wisp of stray hair.

He removed the shovel and the turf ax from the barrow before tilting the barrow onto its side. Lifting Amanda by the hands and then, enduring her cold embrace, by the shoulders, he half dragged, half rolled her into it. In the thirty or so minutes it had taken him to fetch the wheelbarrow from the screenhouse her body had undergone a number of subtle changes. Her skin had taken on a bluish tint; her fingers, though not yet stiffened, felt clammy, like links of raw sausage left overnight on a countertop.

He stood gazing at her, at the lifeless thing she now was, until he could bear seeing her like that no longer, then knelt onto the ground as if in prayer, and with straining muscles pried the barrow and its limp burden upright. The barrow—oversized and constructed of wood, used in his grandfather's day for hauling sand onto the bogs—tottered for a moment, as if it would spill its contents back onto the ground so that he would have to kneel and repeat the process, lift the body into the barrow and then the barrow with the body

3

in it, again and again, condemned for all of eternity to the Sisyphean task of tucking Amanda into the barrow and getting the barrow, and the dead weight in it, upright.

But in the end, as if assisted by demonic hands, the barrow seemed to right itself, and held steady on the rough ground. Like a conscientious workman preparing for an honest day's labor, he retrieved the tools and arranged them, one on each side of her. That task accomplished, he stood squarely behind the wheelbarrow and with a firm grip on each of the bare wooden handles pushed away from the stone wall onto the deserted road. There the hard-packed gravel, studded with pebbles and pocked with holes, hindered momentum; he had to lean into the barrow in order to propel it forward.

Head lolling, arms dangling over the sides, Amanda might have been mistaken for a passed-out drunkard being trundled home.

The barrow's worn rubber tire, grown soft from years of neglect, made the work difficult; the axle, long ungreased, squeaked in protest. Within minutes blisters sprouted on his palms, and he found himself short of breath. From time to time he heard noises in the woods, faint rustlings that might have been an animal, or only the wind. Meanwhile, like the chorus in an ancient Greek tragedy, spring peepers in the surrounding swamp provided a sound effect all their own.

He had not thought to grab a flashlight from the screenhouse. No matter; the moon gave ample light. Nor was he a stranger to this neck of the woods. The dirt track upon which he struggled was one he had traversed before, numerous times, part of a network of ancient trails and cart paths, some dating as far back as the first generation of Pilgrims (and before that, too, old Indian trails), that cut through the swamps and uplands, linking the various cranberry bogs for miles.

The section of bog which he had selected for his destination lay just ahead.

Despite a chill breeze and the fact that he had neglected to put on a jacket, he was sweating by the time he reached the grass clearing that bordered the bog. With a sigh, half of anguish, half relief, he released the handles of the wheelbarrow, letting it drop with a dull thud onto its rear supports. The motion jarred its contents; shovel and turf ax rattled against the wooden sides. Wide-eyed, Amanda gazed up at him in seeming reproach.

Returning the corpse-stare, he felt a wave of revulsion. This was followed immediately by a spate of self-pity. He was not the man for this task; he lacked the necessary nerve. And yet…he had come this far. There could be no turning back. Without allowing himself further reflection he toppled the barrow onto its side, spilling body and tools onto the sod. The shovel and the turf ax fell clear of the barrow. Amanda remained partially inside, like an accident victim half ejected, with the rim of the overturned barrow athwart her torso. He seized her ankles and tugged her free.

It was a needless cruelty, he realized, even as he performed it: to treat her so. He could simply have lifted the barrow away from her.

He was not thinking properly.

He pulled a clean, neatly folded white handkerchief from his pants pocket and mopped his brow. It was a delaying action; he did not relish the next phase of the ordeal and wished to put it off, if only for a moment or two. Well, there were the tools to be dealt with. He picked up the shovel and heaved it across the shore ditch onto the bog, then did the same with the turf ax. The head of the ax struck the tip of the shovel with a clatter loud enough to…what? Waken the dead?

All the while the moon, like a lantern held aloft by an angry fist, shone directly overhead.

Having nudged the clouds from the sky, the breeze rattled the bare branches of the trees in the surrounding swamp. The peepers kept up their chorus. He stood at the edge of the clearing that separated the bog from the swamp, uncertain as to the best way to proceed, and felt keenly the wind's bitter bite. With a shiver brought on by revulsion as much as by the chill, he again took hold of Amanda's ankles and dragged her to within a foot of the narrow ditch that separated cranberry bog from upland. For lack of a better plan he rolled her over the lip of the clearing, letting her tumble down the slight embankment into the stagnant water, where, face down, she floated half submerged, like the waterlogged carcass of some poor drowned creature.

He leapt across the ditch onto the cranberry vines below, landing, despite the three and-one-half-foot drop, square on his feet, his fall cushioned by the soft carpet created by the low-growing vines. He reached into the water, took hold of Amanda's head, and yanked her—still face down—onto the bog. Droplets of dirty ditch water adhered to her exposed flesh like bloodsucking leeches unwilling to let go. Contact with the water stung his lacerated palms, rubbed raw by the friction of the barrow's wooden handles.

As if in supplication to an aloof and vengeful deity, he brought his palms upward, and in the moonlight examined the torn blisters. Not used to pain, he felt almost disappointed—as if cheated of potential suffering—to see but slight damage to the skin. These minor abrasions were no stigmata. If anything the moist blisters looked like spent apple blossoms that, loosened by a gentle breeze, had drifted groundward, there to be dampened by the evening dew.

Hardly cause for whining or complaint.

And yet, might not organisms in the filthy water cause infection? He was, after all, a long way off from any washing of hands. If so, it was the least of his worries. Gruesome work—work that before this night was over would leave his hands all the sorer—lay ahead.

He raised a foot over Amanda, straddling her body so that her legs lay between his. Thus positioned, he bent forward as if to engage in an act of necrophilia, but instead bent down to take hold of her calves and dragged her, face down, toward the center of the bog. He advanced only a few feet before halting. Why it should matter now was a question beyond reckoning, yet he could not bear the knowledge of the face he had once loved, the visage he had in moments of transport smothered with kisses, being bruised and sullied, scratched and torn by the tough cranberry vines.

He flipped her over, onto her back, so that the back of her head would bear the brunt of this, her final journey. He avoided looking at her, especially into her eyes. If he could have finished the night's work with his own eyes sealed, he would have done so. No, he was not equal to this…but he had to be, he had no choice, so without further dawdling he resumed the task, and with a supreme effort of will dragged Amanda all the way to the center of the bog.

The temptation now was to leave her there, to quit the bog, to head back through the woods to the house and wash his hands—literally, figuratively—of the whole sordid business. But such folly would negate all that he had accomplished thus far. It was stupid—and dangerous—to even think such things.

He left her, but only temporarily. To complete the task ahead of him he needed the proper tools.

He went back to the edge of the bog in search of the shovel and turf ax. They proved easy to spot in the moonlight; though their metal parts bore the patina of rust, their sturdy ash handles, worn slick by the grasps of generations of robust hands, glinted atop the burgeoning vines like the sun-bleached bones of some long-legged beast.

This night's work would remove the rust from the metal, a goodly portion at least, making the surface shiny once more.

If only conscience were as readily burnished.

Standing there on the sunken field, a tool propped in each hand, he imagined what he must look like: the model for a new and improved American Gothic. Once more he felt a sudden chill. Though their chorus seemed to have grown more distant—as if repulsed by his deed they had moved away—the spring peepers continued to fill the air with background noise, their melodious voices a mockery of silver bells. The peepers closest to him, in the vernal pools of the nearby swamps, had fallen silent. He thought he heard a rustle in the woods. Was it that, that sound perhaps, that had stilled them?

The wind. Only the wind.

And yet something was wrong. Something about the night. Was it the moon, the wanton moon, the way it splashed buckets of yellow liquid all over the bog and its environs? A viscous, indelible light, that would stick, and stain, like guilt? Or was it the peepers—the way they poured out, in unison, their mocking chant, their monotonous trill? He hefted the tools, holding the turf ax in his right hand, the shovel in his left, as if testing their weight, their worthiness, and with a parting glance over his shoulder at the shadows on the upland beyond the bog, trudged back to where Amanda, recumbent like a patient lover on a bed of vines, awaited.

He lay the shovel down next to her, and with the broad blade of the turf ax sliced a six-foot line to one side through the matted vines. Each stroke of the ax cut deep into the yielding soil. At either end of the line, perpendicular to it, he sliced another line, three feet in length, and joined these two with a second six-foot line parallel to the first, forming a rectangle. Having thus marked the grave site, he sliced the turf into smaller units, which he pried loose with the shovel and carefully set aside.

Next he removed the exposed soil, a mixture of sand and humus, to a depth of three feet. For his purposes a shallow grave would suffice. The digging, though ruinous to his flayed palms, proved easy enough, with no tree roots or hidden stumps or buried boulders to contend with. The bog had been flooded all winter, and though the water had been drained off weeks ago, spring rains had kept the soil beneath the low-growing vines soft and spongy.

He paused occasionally to rest and to catch his breath. Although he had lost all track of time, the slow progress of the moon across the night sky hinted that perhaps, at the most, an hour or two had elapsed since the commencement of his excavation.

At last the grave was ready. The site he had chosen—on the spur of the moment—proved ideal for a number of reasons. This was a remote section of cranberry bog entirely surrounded by swamp and wooded upland, with no buildings nearby. More important, both shore and cross ditches had recently been cleared by heavy equipment of built-up sediment and weed growth; the surface of the adjacent vines still showed signs of disturbance. Anyone who chanced by—itself an unlikely occurrence—would hardly notice the further disturbance he was creating by concealing a body. New vine growth would soon obscure even that minor disfigurement. The smooth carpet of tiny pink and white cranberry blossoms due to appear within a few weeks would draw the interest of only the myriads of honeybees foraging from the hives placed for pollination by the beekeeper in strategic locations along the shore.

He turned his attention now to Amanda. She lay stiff and still next to the open grave, her hair in wild disarray, her clothing damp and disheveled—so unlike the voluptuous woman, neat and fastidious to the point of vanity, he had known in life. Stooping, he rolled her into the pit he had dug, where, like a late-night reveler flopping into bed, she came to rest on her side. That would not do. She looked too much asleep. He stepped into the pit and arranged her so that she lay, as if in a coffin, on her back.

There. Much better. If her corpse must suffer the indignity of burial without ceremony, at least let her recline properly. He stood looking down at her, bowed his head in silent prayer—how absurd! he thought—then shoveled the soil he had removed back into the pit and on top of her. When all the soil had been returned and she was completely covered he tamped it down with his shoes to flatten the mound—he should have worn boots for the task, but does one ever properly plan these things?—so that it was packed firmly and evenly.

Next he carefully replaced the blocks of turf—the roots of the vines having suffered little damage—and tamped them down as best he could, so that as the vines put out new growth the rectangular grave site would blend in with its surroundings. With his fingers he raked a few scattered clumps of loose soil into the vines, and was done.

In the stillness that followed, the sound of the peepers swelled through the air like a soulful dirge.

Despite physical discomforts—palms scraped raw and smarting with the salt sting of sweat rubbed in; the frigid embrace of his sweat-drenched shirt; the dull throb in his lower back, portent of worse pain to come—he felt an overall torpor, a numbness akin to—what—battle fatigue? How late was the hour? Or early, if morning had arrived? He glanced at the sky. The moon had by now drifted far to the west; the heavens were studded with stars. There was a serene beauty to the visible universe. An ironic beauty: as if the tinkling of the peepers, those witnesses to his trespass, had crystallized, and each tinkle become a star.

With the turf ax flung like a hobo's bindle stick at a jaunty angle over his shoulder, and the shovel dragging along like a reluctant child at his side, he made his way back to the edge of the bog. One at a time he tossed each of the tools onto shore, then, unencumbered, jumped the ditch and scrambled up the embankment. Like the carapace of a colossal tortoise the upended wheelbarrow awaited him. He righted the barrow, placed the tools inside, and with a thrust that brought new pain to his palms began the weary trek back to the screenhouse.

The merest hint of dawn tainted the eastern sky.

On this, the return trip, the barrow, relieved of its load, jounced over the rough surface with an irregularity that jarred both muscles and nerves. He felt badly in need of a drink—strong spirits: whiskey, rum, anything alcoholic. Such a beverage might, he thought, prove antiseptic to his soul—might prevent spiritual infection—just as antibacterial ointment might help heal the wounds on his hands.

He made his way across the clearing toward the breach in the woods where the hungry maw of the dirt track yawned, eager to swallow him. He had not gone far when he heard sounds of clumsy movement within the brush. That same rustling sound which he had heard earlier, but which he had so cavalierly dismissed? There seemed more volume to it now, a greater intensity, while at the same time a lack of stealth, as if that which had desired concealment no longer felt the need for it.

He came to an abrupt halt. With an ear cocked for clues as to the source of the sounds, he let the barrow rest once again upon its supports. Instinctively he gripped the turf ax, more as a prophylactic against the mounting fear he felt than as a defense against any real danger. Of a sudden, diagonally in front of him, a dark figure emerged from the brush, followed by another, and still another. Others might lurk in the shadows; it was not yet light enough to tell.

The first figure approached him. "We've been watching you," it said.

CHAPTER I
A Feeling of Unease

On an afternoon favored by bright sun and sprightly breeze two women and a cat rested comfortably in a screened-in gazebo that overlooked a cranberry bog in southeastern Massachusetts. It was late spring, and spring itself had come late that year, as it often does in New England.

"'Rough winds do shake the darling buds of May,'" one of the women commented.

"Today is the first day of June," the other reminded her.

Like so many of the cranberry bogs built in the nineteenth century, wrested by ox teams and human brawn from rough swamps and marshy lowlands, this particular bog, a long narrow carpet of sunken vines, was irregular in shape. Ringed in its entirety by a rutted dirt track, it stretched like a shallow inlet of the sea into the distance, until lost to view around a bend. It was, in effect, a pocket of cultivation surrounded by swamp. The more immediate landscape, the grassy clearing on which the gazebo was situated behind a modest Greek revival house, and upland consisting of mixed deciduous trees and white pines, was awash with wildflowers and brimful with avian music.

The trilliums, violets, blue flags, lady slippers, and columbines tossed by the breeze seemed fragile in their airy buoyancy. Less delicate were the bird sounds: the chattering of Carolina wrens, the drumming of red-bellied woodpeckers. Now and then a catbird contributed to the mild cacophony, or a restive titmouse, or a white-breasted nuthatch. All in all it was a tranquil scene, typical of a late spring day, the type of scene upon which only occasionally might violent death intrude.

The women, seated in cushioned chairs with a low table between them, wore light sweaters. The cat, an orange tabby, lay stretched out on the bare cedar floor fast asleep, unperturbed by the sharp bursts of air that, fluffing his fur, exposed tiny patches of pink skin beneath. The breeze, coming as it did from the bog, brought with it the pungent, not unpleasant, smell of stagnant water.

"Is it June already? It feels more like April. Even so, the first day of June is close enough, dear. I'm sure that Shakespeare would forgive me for being one day off." Lena Lombardi leaned over the table and caressed the petals of the red and yellow tulips she had placed in a vase that morning. "Have you made plans for the summer?"

"I may teach one or two composition courses," the younger woman stated. In her mid forties, Cheryl Fernandes was petite, with an olive complexion and dark hair, and a trim figure kept so by prudent diet and exercise; she was professor of English Literature at a local university. "The administration hinted that they'd like me to."

"Do you want to?" Lena asked. "Or would you rather have the summer all to yourself?"

"I'm not sure," Cheryl said.

"Having the summer free would give you extra time to spend with Anthony," Lena said.

"That's what I'm not so sure about," Cheryl confessed. "Anthony's been a sweetheart lately. Perhaps too much so."

"Hinting of marriage?"

Cheryl nodded.

"Once bitten, twice shy," Lena said. "You're wise not to rush into things."

Cheryl cast a wry glance at her companion.

Lena Lombardi, white-haired and in her early seventies, was spry both of body and of mind. She was taller than Cheryl; exposure to sun and wind had wrinkled her skin but not wizened it. Her hazel eyes had, seemingly, a perpetual twinkle to them which betrayed her quirky sense of humor, though those same eyes could with provocation be quick to show anger.

"Anthony and I have been dating for nearly two years now," Cheryl reminded her. "That's hardly 'rushing.'" She reached over and patted the older woman's hand. "I think you just want to keep me here all to yourself."

"Well, of course I do," Lena declared in a huff. "We've been having ever so much fun since you moved in. The three of us," she emphasized, nodding toward the cat. "I mustn't exclude Marmalade; he's grown exceedingly fond of you, and of your cooking, especially your seafood dishes. Besides, you're a positive influence on me."

"Oh? In what way?"

"Why, you keep me in check. I drink much less wine than I used to, hardly a bottle a day. Well, maybe a little over a bottle," she conceded, confronted by her friend's dubious expression. "And I'm not so inclined to stick my nose into other people's business."

Cheryl raised her eyebrows. "No? You could have fooled me."

"Now dear, you know perfectly well I behaved myself all winter," Lena asseverated. "I spent my days reading and watching birds from the window and did absolutely no prying."

"Only because you slipped on the ice and were laid up for six weeks with a sprained ankle," Cheryl pointed out.

"During which time you positively pampered me," Lena said. "Why, at times I felt like Marmalade—shamelessly spoiled." She leaned forward to pluck a tulip from the vase, and idly twirled it between her fingers. Droplets of water clinging to the stem dripped onto the cat's head, causing him to twitch an ear before waking with a start. Annoyed by the impromptu baptism, he brushed a paw over his ear before returning to sleep.

"I sense that you're growing restless," Cheryl observed.

"A bit," Lena said. "I'm eager to get started on a couple of projects. You remember the fat-assed Phyllis, I'm sure?"

"I remember meeting a pleasant woman named Phyllis the day you bought cast-iron frying pans at the Eldredge estate auction, if that's who you mean," Cheryl said.

"That's the very one, dear. I described her to you as being like horse shit: found everywhere. It's an old expression, one I heard when I was a child, when people still remembered the horse-and-

13

buggy days. I keep running into her, in the oddest places."

"That would make you like horse shit, too," Cheryl observed.

Ignoring the gibe, Lena continued: "I ran into her this morning while I was grocery shopping. Her cart was positively loaded with meat—no wonder she's so broad in the beam. Consuming all that animal fat can't be doing her arteries any good—but that's her business, I suppose."

"I suppose," Cheryl echoed, wryly.

"Well dear, you haven't seen her lately, have you? She's grown humungous. I hardly recognized her."

"How'd we get on this subject?" Cheryl wondered aloud.

"Why, *you* ventured the opinion that somehow I seemed restless, and *I* mentioned that I have a couple of projects pending—one of which involves Phyllis. Well, indirectly anyhow."

"Are you planning to put her on a diet?"

"Now dear, don't be a wisenheimer," Lena said pleasantly as she replaced the tulip, its petals somewhat the worse for having been twirled about, into the vase. "I don't mean to be critical of Phyllis; she does have her good qualities. She has a heart to match her butt." Lena paused. "That was a witticism, dear. Though I see you're not laughing."

"This project of yours…" Cheryl prompted.

"I'm getting to that, dear. Phyllis and I got to chatting—poor thing, she does love to gossip! In the course of our conversation the topic of unemployment came up, what with the state of the economy and all, and she happened to mention that a nephew of hers—Brian I believe she said his name is—is looking for work. It seems he's an itinerant carpenter."

"*Itinerant* carpenter?" Cheryl voiced.

"That's how she referred to him," Lena said. "I suppose you could interpret it as a euphemism for 'bum,' though according to Phyllis he's a hard worker. Brian just 'lacks direction' is how she expressed it. He's in his mid twenties. You understand young people better than I do, dear. How is Kristen by the way? Have you heard from her recently?"

"She's doing fine. There was an e-mail waiting for me this morning. She loves her job and her new apartment. Oh, and she hinted that she has a new boyfriend."

"That's nice, dear. You must miss her terribly."

"I do. It's been more than two years now since she left the States."

"You're fortunate to have such a talented daughter. *She* obviously doesn't 'lack direction.' Anyhow, Phyllis insists that this nephew of hers is quite skilled with hammer and saw. Hopefully, skilled enough for what I have in mind."

"And what is that, pray tell?" Cheryl asked, amused at her friend's loquacity.

"The pump house down by the river is badly in need of repair. The floorboards are rotting and the pump shaft doesn't seem all that trustworthy to me. It probably won't take him more than two or three days to fix it up."

"Then you've hired him?"

"Well, not yet, dear. He's supposed to drop by this afternoon. If he seems like a forthright young man I'll give him the job. That way I'll be doing a favor for an old friend. I do like Phyllis, you know, despite her many faults."

"And at the same time you'll avoid having to pay union-scale wages," Cheryl observed.

"Now dear, that's hardly my motive in hiring the young fellow. Though Phyllis did hint that he would not be averse to being paid 'under the table.'"

"Aiding and abetting a tax dodger," Cheryl chided. "You could get yourself into a heap of trouble."

"Nonsense, dear. It's not incumbent upon me to see to it that every Tom, Dick, or Harry who does a day's work for me files an income tax return. Besides, I intend to treat Brian as a private contractor; I'll pay him for the job, not an hourly wage. At least," she added as an afterthought, "he's not one of those undocumented aliens you hear about all the time. Leastwise, I assume he isn't. It wouldn't do to have the Feds raid the place, now would it?"

⁐⁐

It was late afternoon by the time the women left the gazebo and returned to the house. In the mistaken belief that the dinner gong had rung, the cat, tail erect like a ship's mast denuded of sail, scooted eagerly ahead of them.

The trio had hardly settled themselves inside when a small van pulled onto the circular drive in front of the house. Hearing the sound of a door being slammed, Lena went to a window; drawing the curtain aside she squinted through the pane and saw a young man standing uncertainly beside what—letting her imagination run rife—appeared to be a hearse.

Had someone died? Why else would a hearse pull up to her house?

Well, of course no one had died. What utter nonsense! Nor was that a hearse she saw parked in her driveway. Even so, the impression that it might be a hearse, or perhaps a Black Maria, was understandable. Uniformly black, the van, which lacked lettering of any sort, looked as though it might accommodate a human body, a tall one at that, even if it were stretched out to its full length and encased in an oversized coffin. When new and in full sheen the van might very well have passed for a hearse, albeit a compact one; in its present condition, however, it looked anything but prepossessing: certainly not the conveyance a reputable undertaker would care to put a cadaver in.

Lena stood for the longest time peering out. Strangely, she felt unable to pull away, as if she were glued to the window, her hand attached to the curtain—as though it were imperative that she make a full examination, that she take careful note of the van's peculiarities. The original finish, mottled to drabness, showed, where the paint had worn thin, varying shades of gray, not to mention splotches of rust where the paint had vanished completely. Not only was the van in dire need of a new coat of paint, it needed body work as well. Why, it looked more battered than the Ford pickup Lena used for odd jobs around her bog.

No self-respecting corpse would be caught dead in that rattletrap, Lena thought—a witticism she must remember to share with Cheryl, for the latter's delectation.

Much later, toward the end of summer, she would remember her present ponderings and wonder if they had been a premonition of events to come.

⌒⌒

In contrast to the van, the young man who stood next to it seemed positively spiffy, neatly dressed in work clothes that appeared hardly worn, new in fact, fresh off the shelf, as if purchased that very morning.

He was a nice-looking young man, Lena reflected, but heavy-set—if not careful he might end up a male counterpart to his fat-assed aunt—and clean shaven, with no visible tattoos, or metallic ornaments piercing his body. That much was in his favor. Not that Lena was old-fashioned in her thinking. She was—in her own estimation—quite liberal. But she did draw the line at unsightly tattoos (on anyone but a seasoned sailor) and body-piercing, a barbaric custom if ever there was one, abhorrent when practiced by women, ridiculous when practiced by men.

She held her post by the window, waiting for the young man to step onto the portico and knock at her door.

For some reason he seemed reluctant to do so. Shyness? There was something about him that was...how to describe it?...odd. Perhaps he suffered from mental illness. Or had recently been released from an institution. Such a circumstance might account for the newness of his outfit—along with his seeming irresolution, his social awkwardness.

Well, if Mohammed won't come to the mountain, the mountain must go to Mohammed. Is that how the saying went? Or was it the other way around? No matter. With a mental shrug she broke away from the window, opened the door, and walked to the end of the portico.

Immediately the young man stepped forward. "Mrs. Lombardi?"

"You're Brian, I assume," she replied, joining him at ground level. "Phyllis Baker's nephew."

17

He nodded. "Aunt Philly said you might have some work for me."

"I have a pump house in need of repair," Lena said. "Do you know anything about pump houses?"

"I've *built* pump houses. From scratch," Brian said, not without a touch of pride. He went on to name a half dozen local cranberry growers for whom he claimed to have done work.

"Recently?" Lena asked, casting a doubtful eye, first at his off-the-rack outfit, then at the hoary van, with its decorative dings, dents, and nevus-like blemishes.

The young man shrugged but remained silent.

Undeterred, Lena took the initiative. "Wait here while I run inside for a jacket."

When, properly attired, she returned to the van Brian was seated inside with the motor running and the passenger door flung open. She climbed in; not bothering to fasten her seat belt she signaled with a nod for him to proceed along the drive, which wound around to the rear of the house before it linked with the dirt road that skirted the bog.

Rather than proceed immediately, as she expected he would, he hesitated; after an awkward pause he said with an air of embarrassment: "Mrs. Lombardi, would you mind fastening your seat belt?"

At the young man's words Lena was, to put it mildly, taken aback. They were after all on private property, unlikely to encounter another vehicle, or to travel at speeds in excess of fifteen miles an hour. It was as if a chimpanzee, out of the blue, had suddenly suggested a round of golf.

She complied with the request, but chided: "I don't as a rule bother with seat belts around the bog. If you plan on driving recklessly, remember that neither of us is wearing a helmet."

He flushed at her words but waited for the reassuring *click* before releasing the parking brake. Was the pink infusion that spread across his face like an incoming tide indicative of anger? Or embarrassment?

Both, perhaps.

A strange fellow, this nephew of Phyllis Baker, so reticent, so neat, so proper. A young man best treated with circumspection.

A violent lurch—unintentional no doubt, unnerving nonetheless—bucked the vehicle into motion, making Lena thankful, after all, to be belted in. After this less than propitious start Brian drove along slowly, his white-knuckled grip on the steering wheel more characteristic of someone unaccustomed to rutted dirt tracks than a veteran of the bogs. Had he lied to her about his experience? Or was he merely solicitous of the van's low-slung tailpipe and muffler, liable on this rough passage, if he were not careful, to result in costly damage?

"Turn here," Lena said when they reached a fork in the dirt track. The tine to the left continued along the bog, making a full loop around it. The lesser tine, the one she indicated, led through a tunnel of vegetation to the pump house down by the river.

As the young man guided his battle-scarred van along the cart path (you could hardly call it a road), overhanging limbs raked against the roof and sides. Closing her eyes Lena could picture skeletal fingers reaching out, scratching at the passing vehicle: vagrant zombies crowding in, eager for a lift in what they mistook for a hearse to the nearest cemetery.

"I really must attend to this brush," Lena said. "I hadn't realized how overgrown it's become." Despite the implied apology she spoke with a clear conscience; a few additional scrape marks could hardly compromise the van's blemished exterior.

"It does need cutting back," Brian agreed. "I could do it. As part of the job," he added hopefully.

"I suppose so," Lena said. If she awarded him the job in the first place.

Brian parked on a gravel-packed clearing adjacent to the pump house. Without comment he slid from the driver's side and went up to the padlocked door, where he spent a few minutes eyeballing the structure before picking at the peeling paint and running his finger tips along the seams of the boards. Like a worshiper genuflecting before the altar of a pagan god he dropped to his knees and crawled along the foundation before straightening and going over to the side of the building.

"Careful where you step out back," Lena warned. "There's a considerable drop."

He nodded, half listening, the bulk of his concentration devoted to inspection. He rapped his knuckles against the boards, rhythmically, as if conjuring up a tune, then ventured around to the rear, where he stood on the earthen ledge to examine the pump shaft.

Coming around from the other side, Lena stood awhile and observed as heedless of the danger a false step would result in—a headlong plunge to the river—he stooped to the work. She liked the way he probed at the pump house, using only his fingers, like a physician assessing by touch alone his patient's state of health. Leaving him to the task she returned to the door and with her key released the padlock. She swung the door open and hooked it in place to prevent the wind, still gusting, from ripping it off its hinges.

Moments later Brian joined her, pad and paper and tape measure in hand.

As he stepped inside to continue his inspection Lena remained without, to listen to the wind roughhousing through the trees, and the murmur of the stream as it made its slow, winding way down to the sea.

After a short while, five minutes perhaps, Brian emerged, a mantilla of cobwebs pasted to his hair and a displaced spider creeping like an ambulatory stickpin across the front of his shirt. Lena gave the spider a cursory glance—it was harmless, neither a Black Widow nor Brown Recluse—and listened carefully to his estimate of the amount of materials and the length of time it would take to restore the decaying structure.

When he finished she asked a question or two; satisfied with his answers she gave him the nod.

Brian named a price, Lena agreed to it—with an additional sum tossed in for trimming the brush from the edges of the access road—and the pair shook hands, two hardscrabble Yankees clinching a deal. Not until then did Lena call his attention to the spider. Gently, he gave it a fillip with his forefinger, and they climbed into the van.

This time Lena made a point of securing her seat belt.

Brian backed the van in order to turn. Glancing out the window, Lena spotted the exiled spider riding a blade of grass. Would it, inured as it was to the dark recesses of the pump house, blunder through the brilliancy of day only to fall prey to passing bird or toad? Or would it through instinct or luck find its way home, to its accustomed crannies, there once more to enmesh and devour the unwary?

Brian gave the impression, justified she was sure, of being a competent workman, and the price he named was lower than the amount she'd anticipated. All in all she should be feeling quite smug about the transaction. And yet…the notion persisted that all was not what it seemed, that there was something about this young man that was not quite kosher.

For the second time that day she thought of Shakespeare. As they jounced along the dirt track she could not shake the feeling that there was something rotten in the state of Denmark.

CHAPTER II
Missing Pal

On the circular drive an unfamiliar vehicle, a large SUV, sat wedged between Cheryl's car and Lena's two vehicles, her pickup and her sedan. As Brian pulled up to the steps leading to the portico to discharge his passenger a woman got out of the SUV and began walking toward the house. She was clutching something—a bundle of leaflets—in her hand. A man—the driver—and another woman also got out of the SUV but remained standing next to it.

As the woman approached Lena said, more to herself than to Brian, "I know her from somewhere."

"Elizabeth Walderne," the young man said.

"You know her?"

"I've seen her around," he replied. "A cranberry grower. She and her family own bogs across town."

"Ah, that's where I've seen her," Lena said. "At cranberry growers' meetings. Whatever brings her here?" she wondered as she dismounted from the van.

Brian shrugged. Scarcely had Lena slammed the door shut when without a parting word he shifted into gear, and giving Elizabeth Walderne and the SUV a wide berth sped off into the sunset—a strange young man indeed.

"Wasn't that Brian Siminski?" Elizabeth Walderne asked, with a quizzical stare at the van as it swung onto the wooded road and disappeared from view.

"I don't know his last name but his first name is Brian, so I suppose he's Brian Siminski if you say so," Lena replied.

22

Elizabeth looked at her but said nothing.

Fearing that perhaps she had come across as unnecessarily curt, Lena added, in a more friendly manner: "I've hired him to repair my pump house down by the river. You're Elizabeth Walderne, aren't you? We've never formally met, but I know I've seen you at cranberry meetings. Is there something I can help you with?" She cast a doubtful glance at the sheaf which Elizabeth was cradling next to her body, and which the impish wind kept trying to snatch from her.

"Our Pal has gone missing," Elizabeth replied, a sudden quiver in her voice; she appeared visibly upset, as if fighting to hold back tears.

That evening, in her account to Cheryl, Lena would describe Elizabeth Walderne as "big-framed, that is to say, horsy, with a face in harmony with her physique. A suicide blonde—dyed by her own hand. I guess her to be somewhere in her mid to late forties. I only mention this, dear, because her husband—he was with her, along with her sister—looks so much younger and is strikingly handsome. You know, like a movie star. An odd couple. Mismatched. Beauty and the Beast, but with the sexes reversed."

She went on: "The sister looks to be in her thirties. If anything, she's even uglier than Elizabeth. I suppose I'm being unkind—the three of them seemed nice enough, in their own way. From their mannerisms I gathered that they're much more devoted to the missing animal than to one another—anyhow that's the impression I received, in the brief time I was with them, though it may have been due to the great stress they apparently are under. I'd feel the same, of course, if it were Marmalade who was missing. Why, that time when he actually did go missing I was frantic, absolutely beside myself. So I do sympathize with them for being upset, even though it's only a dog that's gone astray, and not a cat."

Elizabeth handed Lena one of the leaflets. Reproduced in color on glossy paper—evidently at considerable expense—it featured a large photograph of a black Lab. To Lena, the Lab looked no different from any of the hundreds of other black Labradors she had encountered in her seventy-plus years, except that in the photo this one was sporting a red bandanna around his neck, which did make him look rather distinguished, dashing almost, in a canine sort of way— as if he had posted his photo on a dating service or Web site for love-lorn dogs: *Single black male, unneutered, seeks unspayed female, one to six years of age, any breed, to share bones, head-out-the-window thrills, intimate sniffing, romps in the woods. "Run wild with me."*

Beneath the photo the dog's name, *Pal*, appeared in bold letters, followed by the word LOST in block letters, with a reward of $1000 promised for the dog's safe return (no questions asked). A street address, a telephone number, and an e-mail address completed the leaflet.

After a polite show of concern by pretending to study the photograph, Lena shook her head. "I'm afraid I haven't seen any stray Labs hereabouts. I'll keep my eyes open of course. Should I hold on to this, just in case?"

"Please do," Elizabeth said. "We're putting them up in shop windows and on signposts and telephone poles all over town. We've had Pal eight years, Mrs. Lombardi. He's a member of the family. I don't know what we'll do if he doesn't turn up."

Get another, I suppose, Lena thought to herself. *They all look alike.* Aloud she said: "I know just how you feel. I'm an animal lover myself."

The man and woman who had thus far held aloof now came over to join them. The man introduced himself as "Harvey Cardozo, Elizabeth Walderne's husband. And this is Marguerite Walderne, Elizabeth's kid sister."

Kid sister? Marguerite Walderne seemed rather long in the tooth—forty years old, if a day—to be referred to as such. And as for Elizabeth—not that Lena herself was in any way old-fashioned; on the contrary, she considered herself a model of feminism—she could not for the life of her understand why a woman who purports to love a man enough to marry him would fail to adopt his last name as her own. Why, the proudest moment in Lena's life was when she became Mrs. Rinaldo Lombardi. Harvey *Cardozo* and Elizabeth *Walderne*: it just didn't sound right. But that, of course, was merely her humble (call it, if you must, 'old-fashioned') opinion.

"He broke loose from his chain two days ago," Harvey Cardozo was explaining, when she returned her attention to the matter at hand. "That is, he slipped his collar. We blame ourselves. We almost never chain him outside. But we had some friends over who don't care for dogs and…" Letting the sentence trail off, he held up his hands in a hopeless gesture.

"But don't you live clear across town? Do you think your dog could have wandered this far?" Lena asked. *And made it here unscathed*, she added mentally, mindful of the hazards the local highways with their Cape Cod-bound traffic posed to humans, let alone to wayward pets.

"We're not all that many miles distant, as the crow flies," Harvey said. "There's really only a few miles of bogs and swampland between there and here."

"Our hope is that Pal cut through the swamps and somehow got lost," Elizabeth said. "He may have been chasing something. A rabbit or a feral cat. Or he may have taken up with another vagabond dog. He could be anywhere out there," she added, indicating the vast area of swampland and cultivated cranberry bogs that began in back of Lena's house and stretched on for miles. "Frightened and hungry." When she finished speaking she began to chew at her large, bulbous lips, calling to mind a grief-stricken hippopotamus.

Though Lena, herself an inveterate cat person, felt sorry for the dog-lovers, as well as empathy for their grief, she wished they would hurry up and leave. Despite the protection afforded by the denim jacket which she had prudently donned before venturing out with Brian, the unseasonable wind chilled her through and through; she longed to return inside, to the comfort of her library, and ignite the stack of logs and kindling which she had earlier in the day neatly arranged in the fireplace. There, in an armchair by the crackling flames, Marmalade at her feet, and her good friend Cheryl to keep her company, she would enjoy a glass or two of red wine. A hearty shiraz, or perhaps a red zinfandel? to warm, if not the cockles of her heart, then at least the marrow of her bones.

Marguerite, who had thus far remained silent, said: "We'll up the reward if we have to—though I honestly don't think it will do much good. Pal is either alive. Or dead. The amount of the reward won't really change anything."

Of the three, Marguerite seemed the most discouraged—or should that be *disillusioned*? while at the same time, though ostensibly saddened, the least upset, causing Lena to wonder just how she came into the picture. Was she there merely to lend moral support? Did she live with her sister and brother-in-law, and if so, was Pal their dog, not hers? And the way she kept eyeing the other two…with sidelong glances…Lena couldn't quite put her finger on it but…was Marguerite resentful in some way of her sister and brother-in-law?

Well, the makeup and inner dynamics of the Cardozo-Walderne ménage were no concern of hers. She understood the depth of their loss, but…if only they would make their departure!

Finally, after further wailing and gnashing of teeth (here Lena admitted to herself that she was being unkind, her insensitivity due in large part to her impatience to return inside) they did depart: a peculiar threesome, two of them, though beginning to despair, not yet entirely bereft of hope; the third seemingly resigned, if not uncaring. As the SUV pulled out of the driveway Lena could almost feel the emptiness within it, the void which the missing Pal, with his tail-wagging presence, would have filled.

"Who were those people you were talking to?" Cheryl asked when Lena returned inside.

Lena handed her the flyer. "Their dog is missing."

"How sad," the younger woman said, gazing at the photo of the star-crossed Pal. "A thousand dollars reward! I must say I'm impressed." Shaking her head she added: "These things, I'm afraid, seldom have happy endings."

"All the more reason to make merry while we may," Lena declared.

"What kind?" Cheryl asked. "Red or white?"

"Now dear, it's positively scary when you read my mind like this!" Retrieving the flyer, she added: "I thought perhaps a nice shiraz. Shall I get a fire going in the library while you fetch the libations?"

"That Brian Siminski is a disturbed young man, I fear," Lena observed, after relating to her friend the events that had transpired between them on their ride to the pump house.

"And yet you hired him."

"I think I hired him," Lena said. "The way he took off like that, without a word of goodbye, has me wondering whether he'll show up in the morning."

"If he needs the work he will," Cheryl reassured her. "What do you think is his problem?"

"I don't know." She applied her lips to the rim of her glass (her second) and took a pensive sip. "And he wasn't the only strange bird I encountered today. Those folks with the missing dog…"

"Now Lena. Just because—in your estimation—the man is nice-looking—"

"Positively handsome," Lena said, cutting off her friend in mid sentence. "And younger than his wife—by a good five years I'd reckon." She nodded sagely. "A good five years. I'd bet the farm on it."

"And—in *your* estimation," Cheryl went on, undaunted by the interruption, "his wife and sister-in-law are rather plain—"

"'Plain,'" Lena interrupted again, "is an understatement. 'Ugly' is the operative word."

"You can be so cruel," Cheryl remonstrated. Leaving her wine untouched, she rose from her chair and paced in front of the fire. "It's a cliché, but evidently you need to be reminded—beauty is only skin deep."

"So it is, dear. But don't forget the corollary: 'Ugliness is to the

27

bone.'" Lena took another sip of wine before adding: "I just can't see the two of them married to each other. It would be as if Marmalade were married to a woodchuck. And the sister-in-law—Marguerite… how does she fit in? She strikes me as being a very bitter woman."

"All this, on the basis of five minutes' conversation?"

"You weren't there, dear, else…"

"Else what?"

"Else you might have found the three of them peculiar, too." She took a healthy swallow of wine, and shrugged. "Then again, who knows? The strangeness I detected in Brian Siminski—his singular behavior—may have carried over and tainted my perception of those three. Or, put another way, it may have primed me to detect oddness where none exists. Am I making sense, dear?"

"About as much sense as you ever do," Cheryl replied, as she left off pacing and reclaimed her chair.

CHAPTER III
Remains To Be Seen

Joe Kelley glanced down at his wrist, at the face of the watch his wife, Sandi, had presented to him two years ago, on the occasion of his fiftieth birthday. When Joe saw the time, his own face broke into a broad grin. It was precisely ten a.m., not a second sooner, not a second later. Was he a natural-born wiz, or what?

Something—some second sense—always told him when it was break time.

Taking his foot off the gas pedal and shifting into neutral, he lowered the blade of the small bulldozer he had been operating since shortly after seven that morning, killed the engine, and using the steel tread as a step, hopped onto the ground.

Although his legs had grown stiff from sitting so long, and the ground underneath felt spongy, even soggy, so that in places he sank all the way up to his ankles, he lost no time in striding across the area he had just stripped and—despite a bum knee that had been giving him trouble for the past couple of months—jumping ashore. Out of habit, though not another human being was in sight, nor was one likely to be, out here in the boondocks, he sought out a clump of bushes before relieving himself.

That done, he sat in the cab of his truck with the door wide open and enjoyed the thermos of coffee and the oatmeal cookies Sandi had packed for him that morning. After the protracted drone of the John Deere, the stillness of the surrounding swamp, broken only by occasional bird song, soothed his senses, reminding him somehow of the body massages Sandi used to give him on a regular basis in the

29

first few years of their marriage, before their sons were born. Those massages used to relax him, to the extent that he would sometimes fall asleep even before she had finished.

Today Mother Nature (assisted by Joe's undiagnosed sleep apnea) was the one with the soporific touch. Despite the caffeine he felt drowsy; he knew that if he leaned back, closed his eyes, and let his mind go blank, the silence would take over, and he could catch forty winks—and who would be the wiser?

But Joe Kelley, honest as the day was long, was scrupulous about time; you could set your watch by Joe. No snoozing on the job for him. At exactly ten fifteen—not a minute later—he took another quick leak behind the bushes and returned to the dozer.

The work was easy but monotonous. This section of cranberry bog was at least a hundred years old. He was stripping it of its original vines—Early Blacks—so that the owner could replace them with one of those new high-yielding varieties. Instead of one hundred barrels of cranberries an acre, the owner would average three hundred, maybe more. In Joe's opinion, the work should have been done in the fall, to get a jump on the growing season the following year. But who was he to say? The company he worked for—and had for the past twenty-two years—paid him well. They paid him to run heavy equipment, not to tell other people how to run their business.

Joe figured he could last without a bathroom break until noon. But his enlarged prostate (like his sleep apnea, undiagnosed) would have it otherwise. All that coffee had an adverse effect. Joe staved off the urge to urinate as long a he could, but around eleven thirty-five he gave up the battle and, lowering the blade, shut off the engine. Under similar circumstances some guys Joe knew from previous jobs he had worked on would simply have stood on the tread, unzipped, and with the wind to their backs pissed over the side.

Not Joe.

Even when alone, with zero likelihood of being observed, Joe's sense of decorum compelled him to dismount, select a spot where he could use the John Deere as a shield, and only then go about the business of emptying his bladder.

While thus engaged he naturally stared at the ground. What was unnatural about the situation today was the creeping sensation that he was not alone, that someone—something—was staring back.

If hollow eye sockets can be said to stare.

CHAPTER IV
Bare Bones

Looking like a dowager duchess holding a dead rodent by the tail, Lena Lombardi let the key to her Ford pickup dangle from her fingers before handing it over to Brian Siminski. Fearful, perhaps, that she might at the last moment change her mind, the young man snatched the proffered key from her hand, and like a circus ape intent upon escape leapt into the cab.

"You'll first want to stop for gas," Lena said as he started the engine. She thrust a pair of twenty dollar bills through the open window. "Give me a chance to remove my arm before you take off like a bat out of hell," she quipped.

He smiled—it was the first time she had seen him do so since their initial meeting—and without further adieu sped off.

It felt strange, watching the tail end of her pickup disappear down the road. She was taking a chance, she knew, letting this impetuous young man (whose only recommendation was the dubious distinction of being Phyllis Baker's nephew) borrow her truck. What if he were to cause an accident? As owner of the vehicle she could be held liable, possibly sued, for any damage, any personal injury, he might cause.

Well, what of it? The odds were (he was, after all, a cautious driver) that he would return safely, mission accomplished. And if he didn't, if he wrecked her truck or, less likely, absconded with it to Mexico or South America, she had adequate insurance to cover her losses, and a second vehicle—her trusty Ford sedan—for transportation.

Mid morning found the septuagenarian bustling about the kitchen, a dozen cranberry muffins, left on the counter to cool, and a cranberry pie, baking in the oven, proof of her industry. In a corner next to the stove, like a mislaid skein of orange yarn, Marmalade lay loosely coiled, tuckered out from his own matinal exertions: the mutilation of a catnip-stuffed cloth mouse, a birthday present from Cheryl. Though his eyes remained shut, distant sounds, audible to the cat but not to the human, caused one ear to lift.

"Lena—you home?" The inquiry issued from the vicinity of the front door.

"In the kitchen, dear." Lena set down the rag with which she had been drying dishes and went into the living room to greet her friend.

"When I didn't see your pickup parked in the driveway I thought you must be out," Cheryl said. "But when I came through the door and caught the aroma of—let me guess, cranberry muffins?—I knew you couldn't be too far afield. As you can see, I've been shopping." She nodded toward a cluster of plastic bags heaped on the floor.

"I let Brian take the pickup," Lena explained. "He drove it bright and early this morning to Lowe's at Wareham Crossing to fetch the material he needs for the repairs to the pump house. He's down by the river now."

"Something wrong with his van?"

"The two-by-fours were a bit long for it, dear."

"So he's turning out okay?" Cheryl asked. She bent over to pat Marmalade who, mindful of the catnip mouse and hopeful of future treats, had unraveled himself from his corner in the kitchen to plod into the living room. "You seemed a little leery at first."

"He does act a little peculiar at times," Lena conceded. "But he did such a splendid job cutting back the brush from the road leading down to the river that I feel I can trust him."

"Would you like me to fix lunch after I put these away?" Cheryl asked as she headed upstairs with her purchases.

"If you don't mind, dear. As your nose has already informed you, I've been baking most of the morning: cranberry muffins and a mock cherry pie. I thought I might take a couple of the muffins down to the river for Brian to have with his lunch, and maybe a piece of the pie. Just as an excuse, you know, to check on how he's doing."

"Just an excuse to pamper him, the way you do Marmalade and me," Cheryl called down with a laugh from her room. Then added: "Just don't invite him to have lunch here with us. You may trust your itinerant carpenter, but I'm not so sure that I do."

Lena waited until the pie had cooled before cutting a huge slab and sliding it into a plastic storage bag. She had already stuffed a similar bag with three oversized muffins. It was after twelve when she arrived in her sedan at the pump house by the river. She found Brian sitting in the doorway. Although he had already eaten lunch he seemed pleased with the gift of pastries, which, he assured her, he would consume, if not with supper that night, then for breakfast the following morning.

The lumber and other construction materials purchased that morning at Lowe's were neatly stacked to one side of the building. Already he had begun to strip away shingles and rotting boards that needed replacing.

Lena was pleased. With no electricity available to power his tools, Brian had to do everything—sawing, drilling, sanding, planing, pounding—the old-fashioned way, by hand. He did so without complaint and, if appearances were not deceptive, with skill and efficiency. Despite his idiosyncrasies, his little quirks of personality, she was beginning to like this young man. Was he Phyllis Baker's nephew by blood? she wondered. Or by marriage? She'd have to ask the old fat-ass, the next time she saw her.

It was a pleasant day, bursting with sunshine, the sky marred only by tiny puffs of clouds like plumped up pillows drifting high overhead. They looked so soft and inviting that Lena could imagine that rapscallion, Marmalade, leaping onto one of them and promptly falling asleep, floating far above the continents to awaken hours later

34

somewhere over Asia, where, as the cloud dissipated, he would float like a feather down to earth. Stranded in a foreign land, he'd have to learn a new language: Mandarin Chinese!

Though come to think of it, weren't the Chinese fond of cats? *Fond* in the culinary sense. She had read somewhere that cat was considered a delicacy in certain parts of China, and was available at restaurants, along with dog, and two types of rat. In some establishments customers were allowed to go out back and select their own dog, cat, or rat from among those held in pens, much as diners on Cape Cod might choose a lobster from among crustaceans kept live in a holding tank. The delicacy would then be killed and prepared before the customer's eyes.

No, it would not do for Marmalade to snooze on a cloud and drift all the way to China!

Anyhow it was a silly notion. Lena resolved not to mention it to Cheryl; her friend considered her whacky enough already.

The day proved so lovely—the only wind a westerly breeze—that she and Cheryl opted to have their lunch in the gazebo.

When the two of them were comfortably seated, with Marmalade securely planted on *terra firma* thousands of miles from the Great Wall, Cheryl lifted the lid of the wicker basket into which she had packed their simple repast.

Lena, leaning forward and peering in, rubbed her hands with delight. "Egg salad sandwiches, with fresh whole grain bread. And lots of fresh red-leaf lettuce. Not to mention a chilled bottle of Chardonnay! Who, I may well ask, is spoiling whom in this household?"

Cheryl smiled but remained silent. She knew perfectly well that even though Lena was sufficiently fond of egg salad sandwiches, it was the wine that prompted the outburst. She reached into the basket and pulled out a plastic container that had once held hummus from Trader Joe's, but which now held Marmalade's lunch, a jumbo bake-stuffed shrimp left over from a recent meal and cut into bite-size pieces. She set the container on the floor; even before it touched the boards Marmalade thrust his nose into it and commenced to chew voraciously.

"Now that you know you won't be teaching this summer, have

35

you formed any definite plans?" Lena asked, after the two had consumed their sandwiches but still had a smidgen of Chardonnay to enjoy.

Cheryl nodded. "I've made up my mind to get on with my book on local folklore. I've put it off long enough. I just need to find a unifying theme."

Lena thought for a moment. "If you want my opinion, dear," she finally said, "folklore, however local, is much too broad a subject. You ought to narrow it down."

"Hmm. You may have something there. Narrow it how?"

Lena reached for the bottle, which like a precious *objet d'art* held position of honor between them; there was no need for an ice bucket, since no uncorked wine ever survived long enough to lose its chill. She dribbled the few remaining drops into Cheryl's glass. Only when that task had been completed did she state, flatly: "Cranberries."

Cheryl wrinkled her nose as if attempting to suppress a sneeze, then burst out laughing.

"Did I say something funny, dear?" the older woman asked.

Cheryl attempted to appear contrite. "I'm sorry, Lena; it's just that I expect you to suggest something in the order of haunted houses, or witches, or herbal potions, and what comes out of your mouth is 'cranberries.'"

"And why not cranberries?" Lena asked, indignant. "Aren't cranberries indigenous to this area?"

"I don't suppose a great deal has been done on the subject," Cheryl conceded. "Certainly not a full-length book."

"Any number of legends have grown up around the bogs. Why, to get you started you have Joe Baker."

"The ghost who haunts your screenhouse? I'd forgotten all about poor old Joe." She took a ruminative sip from her glass. "There's no doubt that bogs can be mysterious. Why, just this morning I heard something on the radio about human remains—a skeleton—being found on a bog right here in town."

At Cheryl's words Lena lost her equipoise and shot up from her seat with a movement so sudden it caused a crick in her neck (which would trouble her for days) and greatly startled Marmalade.

36

"A human skeleton? Here in town?"

"If I heard correctly," Cheryl said.

"Whose could it be?" Lena wondered. "The bones of a Native American no doubt. Growers used to build their bogs wherever it was convenient, with total disregard for Indian burial sites. Or the bones could be those of a settler killed in King Philip's War. Now, that would be an historic find!"

"I didn't get the impression that the bones are old," Cheryl said. "Truthfully, at the time I wasn't paying much attention."

"Whose bog? Did they say?"

Cheryl shook her head. "If they did, I didn't catch the name. Just that it was off in the woods somewhere."

"It's times like these that I regret not owning a television," Lena said. "I suppose I'll have to go out and buy a newspaper. I wonder…"

Cheryl cast a suspicious glance at her friend. "Do you have an inkling as to whose bones they may be? Has someone you know gone missing?"

"No one I know personally, dear. But five or six years ago—no, it must be closer to ten, now that I think of it; time passes so quickly—a young woman in town named Amanda Verfurth went missing. That is to say, she disappeared apparently without a trace. It was in all the media at the time. Of course everyone suspected her husband. But without a body, or other evidence…A skeleton on a cranberry bog. It could be Amanda's."

Lowering her fingertips, Lena gently scratched behind Marmalade's ears.

CHAPTER V
A Sad Story Told

Lena Lombardi hummed softly to herself as she strolled along the grassy perimeter of her cranberry bog. Despite a tinge of arthritis in her joints—just a tinge, especially in her right knee, and of course that crick in her neck—she was in fine fettle. How could she not be, given the landscape, the Impressionistic palette with which Mother Nature had painted this glorious June day: the sky a robin's-egg blue; the flowers a rainbow of pinks, whites, purples, and yellows; the unfurled tree leaves burgeoning into a thousand hues of green. Even the sight of a brazen muskrat schooning along a main ditch, and she without her .22, failed to dispel her feeling of well-being. There would be time enough, some other day, to play Grim Reaper to this pesky member of the rodent clan, this vandalizing vole, this destroyer of dikes, this sapper, this tunneler, this underminer of earthen works, this saboteur of sod and turf.

And indeed there will be time...to murder and create. Yes, time enough, some other day, to murder muskrats. And create...what? A void where once a vole had been?

Ah, but there was yet another reason, besides the splendid artistry of her natural surroundings, to explain Lena's jubilation, her unbounded euphoria, her recitation of T. S. Eliot.

A skeleton unearthed.

Just think: an unsolved mystery, almost in her own back yard. Well, clear across town. But still! A cold case, hot again! The media were abuzz with it.

Lena did not own a television set, nor was she connected to the

Internet. But she did own a radio, more than one. And she did buy newspapers, occasionally. Besides, Cheryl owned a computer—she had to, because of her teaching position at Bridgewater State University—and was well versed in what were to Lena the intricacies, the arcana, of the great World Wide Web, including access to the latest breaking news. And to top it all off, Lena was acquainted with a number of women who, charitably, could only be called gossips. You might say that she had her own Internet, or Web. All she had to do was pick up the phone...

That morning she had been on the phone with Phyllis Baker.

"Of course it was the husband. Who else?" Phyllis had insisted, with her usual pigheadedness.

"Now, Phyllis, we don't know that for a fact." She paused. "The police don't have any real evidence pointing to him, do they?"

"What more evidence do they need? She was found—what's left of her—buried on his cranberry bog. The police aren't saying much, but *I* heard (I can't reveal my source, but it's someone who works for the town) that her skull showed evidence of blunt trauma. In other words he whacked her one, with something, a baseball bat or golf club or whatever, then carted her off to one of his cranberry bogs—he owns quite a few, you know; at least one of them is deep in the swamp—and buried her in a shallow grave. Brilliant, when you think of it. Who would have thought to look for her body there?"

Wanting to pump Phyllis further (the woman, like a woodtick firmly attached to a dog's ear and bloated with its blood, was bloated with information) and wishing not to antagonize her, Lena refrained from stating, or rather, asking, the obvious: why, if Kurt Verfurth had murdered his wife and buried her on a remote section of cranberry bog, would he, ten years later, have the vines on that same bog stripped by a bulldozer in order to replace them with a newly developed variety? Was he so reckless, that he did not care if the bones were revealed? That made no sense.

Phyllis Baker was not the sharpest knife in the drawer. But it would do no harm to humor her. After all much can be learned, even from a fool, by professing ignorance.

"What was his motive, do you think?" Lena asked. "I mean, for killing his own wife. Judging by her picture in the paper, Amanda Verfurth was a very attractive woman. And so young. Only twenty-five when she disappeared."

"I suppose you could call her attractive," Phyllis conceded, grudgingly. "Kind of skinny, I always thought. Almost anorexic."

A pregnant hippo would look anorexic if it stood next to you, Lena thought, but held her peace. Aloud she said: "Then you knew her?"

"Only slightly. That is to say, by sight." Then she added something which, evidently, she had been eager to say all along: "She was nothing but a tramp. Little better than a trollop."

"You mean she 'ran around'?" Lena ventured.

"That's exactly what I mean. *Before* she got married. And *afterward*. Her husband was older than her, by I'd say a good fifteen years. And nothing to look at. Mean tempered, too, they say, though I don't know that for a fact. She married him for his money of course. They say he made it in oil. He's from Texas originally. Came to Massachusetts and got it into his head to grow cranberries. Bought up a bunch of little bogs, here and there, and one or two big ones, too. She definitely married him for his money."

"And your theory is that he found out about her infidelities, and killed her out of jealousy?"

"Jealousy or rage. Something like that. Why, it's obvious."

"You don't think one of her lovers might have killed her? Out of jealousy perhaps, if she had more than one paramour, or if she refused to leave her husband."

"And then buried her on a section of one of her husband's cranberry bogs? I suppose it's possible—but it would have to be someone who knows the area well. The bog they found her on is out in the middle of nowhere. No, I think *he* killed her. Now that I recall, he was a good deal shorter than her—by at least three inches. That makes a difference, you know—a man shorter than his wife. They looked ridiculous together. *He* killed her. He might have even planned the murder well in advance. That's only my humble opinion, of course."

Humble indeed. "You think it might have been premeditated?"

"I'm only guessing. But it's awful suspicious, the way the wife disappeared on a night when her husband conveniently had—supposedly—the perfect alibi." She paused for effect.

"I'm all ears," Lena said encouragingly. *Whereas you, Phyllis dear, are all butt. They don't call you 'fat-assed' for nothing.*

"Amanda Verfurth was last seen on a Saturday. Now, it just so happens that every Saturday afternoon hubby would drive down to the Cape to stay with his elderly father. The old gent, it seems, was in failing health and couldn't be left alone. His son paid for people to come in during the week to care for him but took over himself on weekends. Humph. Probably to get a few hours' relief from his young hussy of a wife!"

"Let me guess," Lena interjected. "Your theory would be that sometime during the night Kurt left his father's place on Cape Cod, snuck back home, dispatched his philandering spouse, buried her on a remote section of bog, then hightailed it back down to the Cape."

"Or never went to the Cape in the first place," Phyllis asserted.

"And if the police questioned the old man, which they certainly would have done, he was too much out of it, from Alzheimer's or some other form of dementia"—*a malady for which, Phyllis dear, you are already exhibiting early symptoms*—"to contradict his son's statements. Am I close?"

"You've hit the nail on the head," Phyllis said with, Lena imagined, a smug smile.

"Well, you could be right about the husband," Lena said. "Then again, if it was generally known that he left for the Cape every Saturday, someone else…"

"Who, your jealous lover?"

Don't take on a superior tone with me, you gravitationally challenged walrus, Lena muttered mentally. Aloud she said: "Not necessarily a jealous lover. It could be a tired or bored or even repentant lover, wishing to extricate himself from the illicit relationship. A married man, perhaps. Amanda might have been making demands, threatening to tell the wife."

"We'll know soon enough," Phyllis said, in something of a huff. "It'll be interesting to see just how long it takes the police to make an arrest."

As a member in good standing of the Cape Cod Cranberry

Growers' Association, Lena knew—if only by name—most of the local bog owners, Kurt Verfurth among them. Ten years ago the responsibilities of managing a midsize cranberry bog, together with the routine tasks of daily living, had taken up the bulk of her time; she had felt little more than idle curiosity toward the circumstances of his wife's disappearance.

However, now that with the arrival of her "golden years" (how she loathed that euphemism!) she had relinquished direct oversight of her bog to a growers' service, she found that she had much free time on her hands. What harm could there be in devoting a tiny portion of that time to following the latest scandal?

"Let me know if there are any further developments in the case," she said to Phyllis, before changing the subject.

When she set out from the house it was with the intention of walking clear down to the river, to see how far Brian had progressed with his work on the pump house. Halfway there she changed her mind. It had been a while since she had last set foot in her screenhouse; the notion occurred to her that the century-old building might be in need of repair—something Brian could attend to, once he finished sprucing up the pump house.

However, as she approached the screenhouse her purpose was once again subverted, not by indecision, but by the sight of scavengers bunched in the sky. A mile or so beyond the clearing where the hoary edifice sat overlooking the bog, a half dozen turkey vultures drifted, on tilted wings, in a loose cluster above the trees, each bird a grim speck against the pervasive blue. To her imagination, it was as if snippets of fabric had been torn from the sky, allowing the void of outer reaches to show through.

It was not unusual to see turkey vultures silhouetted above the swamp. Connoisseurs of decay, they were drawn to corruption; the scent of death was sweet to them. And death, from predator or disease, was a frequent visitor to the swamp. But to see more than two or three vultures at once, now that *was* a bit out of the ordinary.

Even as she watched, a seventh vulture, a black mote at first, then an ill-defined blot, came gradually into view. What could be the culinary magnet for so many buzzards? Surely not the remnants of a coyote kill, or the paltry scraps left by a fox. To draw such a crowd this *table d' hôte* must be something greater, a carrion cornucopia, the carcass of some large animal.

No concern of hers, of course. Except…

With forbodings, and berating herself for a fool, she skirted the screenhouse and plunged through the tangle of undergrowth into the swamp. She was no stranger to the terrain; she had lived here as an adult for half a century, had known the area before that in childhood, had explored it regularly, knew all its nooks and crannies, all the animal trails, the old Indian trails, where the best high bush blueberries were, where cold-water springs bubbled up from the ground, where not to tread for fear of sinking waist-deep into muck. She knew of other dangers, too: woodticks, deer ticks and the diseases they carried; the various poison ivies, oaks, and sumacs; mosquitoes bearing West Nile Virus, and worse, most deadly of all, Eastern Equine Encephalitis.

Pshaw! You could pick up any of those nasty items in your own back yard, just strolling along, or gardening, or mowing the lawn.

She crossed what remained of an old Pilgrim road (or so she imagined it was, though it may have dated from a generation or two later), abandoned now for a hundred years, only the faintest traces of twin ruts to show that ox-drawn carts and horse-drawn wagons had once passed there routinely. To avoid lacerations she picked her way carefully, through dense brush and bull briars coiled like barbed wire, toward a clearing she knew of, where, she surmised, the thing was that had whetted the appetite of so many turkey vultures.

She came upon the scene abruptly, a small clearing that was in actuality a vernal pool. In the drought of summer its waters would go dry; now they still retained a depth of several inches.

The vultures had already descended, like so many grief counselors.

They were ugly birds, loathsome even, though necessary she knew to a healthy environment. They were nature's sanitation workers. Like undertakers, or diners invited to a formal banquet, they wore black. They shrugged their wings at her approach, and at the very last moment lifted into the air, coming to roost in low-hanging branches closeby. They seemed to know, or at least intuit, that she was no rival for their repast, that the intrusion was but momentary. They waited with hunchbacked patience, the dinner party who have arrived on time but whose table is not quite ready.

The guest of honor was dressed all in black, too. Poor Pal. He did not appear to have been dead long, less than twenty-four hours. A gaping wound on his flank told the sad story, of a dog who had slipped his collar, dashed off on a wild adventure, enjoyed a brief spree, an orgy of scents and sounds, only to be struck by a car and, mortally wounded, crawl off into the woods to die.

CHAPTER VI
The Diary…

Dear Diary:

It has been quite some time now since I have made an entry with substance, one might even say heft—so unlike the insipid jottings that have "captured" the drab happenings of the past decade. I have, I confess, been holding back. I have not confided in you the way I used to. Why make a record of my innermost thoughts? Why a recital of my innermost feelings? In this life—such as it is—it is deeds that matter, not thoughts, not feelings.

Besides, long ago I ceased to feel comfortable recording my intimate secrets, in ink, on the pages of an impersonal entity such as yourself, an entity over which I have little control—that is to say, upon whose discretion I cannot depend.

You are, after all, an inanimate being, a mere physical object, a thing; you are composed of atoms and molecules. Though you can be hidden under cover, tucked away, concealed in some deep, foul recess (or, more daringly, more cleverly, like Poe's purloined letter, in a conspicuous place), you cannot be made invisible. Suppose some blundering fool, by the merest chance, should stumble upon you? What then? You cannot be made to self-destruct, to blanken your pages.

You do understand my need for caution?

I will tell you this much (else why am I composing this entry?): I have a secret, a secret which even you don't know. It is a secret I have held close to my heart for a long, long time. How much longer I hold it depends...

CHAPTER VII
Smorgasbord

When she phoned the dog's owners to inform them of her grim discovery, Lena had expected whoever took the call to react with sorrow, thank her for her trouble, possibly offer her the reward (which of course she would refuse), then hang up and be done with it.

She hadn't figured on Elizabeth Walderne-Cardozo's inconsolable grief.

It was Elizabeth who picked up the phone, on the first ring. "Yes?" she mouthed anxiously. "Yes?"

Lena pictured the woman, red-nosed and bleary-eyed, anchored to the phone, a box of tissues at hand, on round-the-clock vigil since the dog's disappearance.

Lena identified herself. "I'm afraid I have bad news," she said. "About your dog, Pal. I've found his body. In the woods." She omitted details of the discovery—the vultures; the raw, gaping wound; the faint but distinct odor of corruption—merely stating that the location was not easily accessible.

"Are you sure it's our Pal?" Harvey Cardozo asked, taking the phone from his wife. Lena could hear the woman's soft blubberings in the background.

"It's a black Lab," she stated flatly.

"Well, it has to be Pal," Harvey conceded. "We'll want to positively identify him, of course, and retrieve the body."

Lena tried to explain that retrieving the body was hardly feasible. "He's deep in the swamp. However he found his way there, there's no discernible trail from my property. I had all I could do to force

47

my way in and out; the area is overgrown with briars and poison ivy. I don't see how you could expect to lug something as large as a Lab out. Or frankly, why you would want to."

"We can't just leave his body there. Exposed to…whatever. I know it's an imposition, Mrs. Lombardi, but it would mean an awful lot to my wife and me, and my wife's sister, if you could point out the spot to us so that we can…somehow get him out."

Lena had been looking forward to relaxing in the gazebo with a glass of wine—just the one glass, mind you—while waiting for Cheryl to return home for supper. She was no stranger to hiking through the woods; a favorite pastime of hers was, and had been for many years, to take long nature rambles over hill and dale. But she was getting on in years—seventy-four her next birthday—and this afternoon's stroll, with its unexpected conclusion, had been arduous and somewhat tiring. She had had more than her fair share of exercise for one day.

And yet, common decency…

When the SUV arrived in her driveway, Lena was there to greet it. She declined Harvey's invitation to climb in, opting instead to lead the way to the screenhouse in her pickup. She was not as a rule squeamish, having, in the vagaries and vicissitudes of her long life, encountered death in its many guises; but if the dog's owners did succeed in extricating the carcass from what, in her estimation, should have been its final resting place in the swamp, she would prefer not to share with it the ride back to her house.

The way to the screenhouse led past the entrance to the narrow byroad, cleared now of encroaching brush by Brian Siminski, that wound down to the pump house. Just as Lena and the closely following SUV passed the entrance, Brian's van emerged, the young man apparently done for the day. In her rearview mirror Lena saw the van nudge to the edge of the road, where it hesitated; rather than take the left that would lead by her house and out to the main road, it swung right, into the wake of the SUV.

Perhaps he has something to communicate, Lena thought.

Within a few minutes the motorcade came to a stop in front of the screenhouse.

"I've just got off the phone with Angel View," Harvey informed Lena, referring to the local pet cemetery. He, his wife, and his sister-in-law, Marguerite, had piled out of the SUV in front of the screen-house and were now looking to Lena for guidance. "They're ready to receive Pal as soon as we can get him there."

"It'll be a comfort, laying him to rest with dignity and the knowledge that we can visit him any time we want to," Elizabeth added tearfully.

Lena's nod was noncommittal. She, personally, could not see the point of buying a plot in which to bury an animal. Devoted as she was to Marmalade, if—heaven forbid—he were to predecease her, she would simply inter him in a shallow, unmarked grave somewhere in the back yard. Why, as much as she had loved her late husband, and still revered his memory—still missed him sorely, after all these years—she seldom if ever visited his grave.

Funerals and cemeteries were for the living, to help them get over their grief and sense of loss, not for the dead, who were beyond caring.

"If you could just point out…" Harvey said, tentatively.

Lena indicated the dense brush behind the screenhouse, and gazed meaningfully upwards, at a pair of circling vultures.

"We'll manage," Harvey said, nodding his head as if to convince, not only Lena, but himself as well. He opened the back of the SUV and slid out a rectangular section of paint-stained tarpaulin, on top of which rode a folded bed sheet.

Marguerite Walderne, like a *maître d'* about to escort a group of diners to their table, stepped forward and taking the bed sheet, cradled it under her arm. The comparison, however, only went so far. She was wearing a most un-*maître d'* plaid flannel shirt and a pair of no-nonsense slacks tucked into sturdy hiking boots. Her face and hands, deeply tanned, were consistent with someone who, whatever the season, spends a great deal of time outdoors—someone equal to the task at hand. Her coarse, plain features remained expressionless as she waited for her brother-in-law to take the initiative.

Harvey Cardozo draped the tarpaulin over his shoulder and looked uncertainly at his wife.

It was obvious that Elizabeth Walderne-Cardozo, unlike her "kid" sister, Marguerite, was nowise prepared for, nor equal to, the task at hand. Frazzled, she stood to one side, pasty-faced, looking for all the world like a bloated zombie—a corpse reanimated beyond its prime, dug up too late, decay having already set in—in a frumpy floral-patterned dress that contrasted harshly with her blowzy features: no proper garb in which to venture into the woods, never mind a New England swamp. Her shoes were what women who intend to spend the greater portion of the day shopping refer to as "sensible." Considering the rough terrain in which the carcass of her beloved dog lay, "ridiculous" would be more apropos.

And yet Harvey stood looking uncertainly at Elizabeth; it was unclear to Lena just what it was he expected of her.

His wife's blessing on the enterprise? Her permission to sally forth?

Lena turned when she heard the sound of a car door slamming shut behind her. Brian had gotten out of his van and was approaching, a questioning glance directed toward his employer. Less than halfway to where she stood he halted and held himself aloof, as if too shy to continue. Lena motioned him over; when he was within earshot she briefly explained the situation, and on impulse asked if he might be willing to assist Harvey and Marguerite in their sad mission.

"I'm sure that Mr. Cardozo and Miss Walderne are perfectly capable of carrying poor Pal out on their own," she said, diplomatically. "But with your help it would be that much easier."

Brian looked at the tarpaulin, then at Marguerite, before shifting his gaze to Harvey. He raised his eyebrows, as if to say, "Well?"

Harvey bit his lower lip and stared at the ground. He seemed ill at ease, as if resentful of this intrusion into what he may have thought as strictly a family matter.

It was Elizabeth who broke the awkward silence. "We would welcome any assistance you can give us, Mr. Siminski."

"Another pair of hands would definitely make our task so much easier," Marguerite seconded.

"Well, then," Harvey said, with a heartiness that seemed somewhat forced, "if we follow a straight line"—he glanced meaningfully at the circling vultures—"we should find him okay." He looked to Lena for confirmation.

She nodded. "The going is rough but not impossible."

If Harvey was hopeful that she might, after all, offer to lead them in, he was in for disappointment. She was simply too tired and—in all honesty—too unsympathetic, to trudge a second time over difficult terrain, to do what the vultures were by their fondness for carrion already doing: showing where the body lay.

Without another word Harvey entered the brush, through an opening which Lena had, by frequent passage in days gone by, kept clear of vegetation. It had been her wont to take this shortcut, though in a different direction from where the carcass lay, to visit her closest neighbors, the Eldredges, when they were alive, and also in season to pick wild blueberries. She knew where the highest concentration of high-bush berries were; she never failed, even in the poorest years, to fill her bucket at least a half dozen times.

She looked forward to blueberry season again this year—just a month or so away. She would whip up a batch of muffins—and a pie, too, why not?—for young Brian, whether he was still employed by her or not: her way of saying thank you, a lagniappe, for his working hard and doing such a fine job.

With nary a glance toward her sister, Marguerite fell in step behind her brother-in-law. Brian was less quick to move—as if he was willing to follow, but not to lead. When he, too, had disappeared into the woods, Lena turned to Elizabeth. The woman just stood there, in utter bewilderment, like the dazed survivor of an earthquake or other natural disaster, still too much in shock to have a clue as to what was taking place.

Lena said: "It'll take them awhile. You'll probably want to wait in your SUV."

She headed for the pickup; there was no sense wasting time just hanging around. It was, after all, not a human being whose body they would be carrying out of the woods. Merely a dead canine. Besides, that glass of wine which earlier she had promised herself had begun to send up distress signals.

Where art thou, o oenophile?

"Mrs. Lombardi…"

"Yes?" inquired the preoccupied Lena: should she choose a nice Chianti, or an equally nice Pinot Noir?

Elizabeth took a faltering step toward her. The woman looked pathetic, at the same time comical, like an obese toddler shunted aside by indifferent caregivers, unwanted and unloved, yet determined to learn how to walk nonetheless. Her blubbery face, wet with tears, enhanced the image.

God, Lena thought, *all I need now is for her to soil her underpants.*

Chin jutted forth, the overgrown toddler, ugly but defiant, came up to Lena and inquired in a querulous voice: "Do you think we could wait—together—in your pickup?" Her lips quivered as she spoke, as if she expected a scolding for being ever so naughty.

"Why, of course, Mrs. uh, Walderne-Cardozo. Or we could go into the screenhouse if you prefer, where it's roomier and much more cozy."

"Oh, no thank you. The pickup will be fine. I just…don't care to be left alone right now. I hope you understand."

"Of course I do." *Don't* she amended to herself. Actually, though, perhaps Lena did understand. Or thought she did. Could guess, anyhow.

The woman was truly an object of pity. Lena knew—from having queried that encyclopedic compendium of town gossip, Phyllis Baker—that Elizabeth and Harvey were childless, and that Marguerite lived with them, in a house the sisters had inherited from their parents, along with many acres—just how many acres, Phyllis could not say—of cranberry bogs and upland. It was a common assumption, Phyllis asserted, that Harvey ("Handsome Harvey" he had been called in his salad days, the heart throb of many a hapless lass) had married the much older (and far from attractive) Elizabeth for her money. The awkward and equally unattractive "kid" sister (according to Phyllis, "a born spinster if ever there was one") came as part of the deal.

52

"Who knows what goes on in that house," Phyllis had hinted, darkly.

Probably not much of anything, Lena thought, judging by the trio's evident dependence on the now deceased Lab. Pal, Lena guessed, had been the emotive center, the psychic glue, that held the dysfunctional threesome together. If not for Harvey or Marguerite, then certainly for Elizabeth. The three had, to one extent or another, doted on the dog, if not on one another. No wonder Elizabeth was disconsolate.

Lena, ever the perfect hostess, graciously opened the passenger door so that Elizabeth could heave herself inside. The woman was not what you would call grossly obese, certainly not by today's super-size standards, no contender for the title of "fat-assed queen" currently held by Phyllis Baker. Even so, she made it a tight squeeze, so that Lena, propped behind the steering wheel and subjected to a succession of soggy sniffles, regretted not having insisted on the screenhouse in which to wait for what, sardonically, she thought of as the funeral entourage.

Lena had parked the pickup so that the cab pointed toward the small clearing in the swamp where Pal, or what remained of him, reposed. The vultures continued to mark the spot by circling high overhead, occasionally dropping down—to sample the buffet, Lena supposed.

Elizabeth seemed oblivious to the vultures, and to what their presence signified. Unlike her sister, Marguerite, she did not appear to be the outdoorsy type. Lena had known women like her before. Raised in the country, they might as well have been city bred, for all they understood of nature. They spent much of their time indoors, in front of a television, at a computer, on the phone, or in shopping malls. If they ventured outside, it was to fetch the mail, though they would most likely do that by stretching an arm through the open window of an automobile, rather than actually walk the short distance from the house to the mailbox.

To distract Elizabeth from her distress (and hopefully put an end to that incessant sniffling), Lena brought up the subject of the skeleton that had recently been unearthed on the cranberry bog across town.

"Not far from where you live," Lena commented.

"Near one of our bogs," Elizabeth said. "Kurt Verfurth's property, where the bones were found, abuts ours. Way back in the woods of course."

"Did you know the dead woman? Amanda?"

"Slightly. She lived—Kurt still lives—a couple of miles from us. We're all cranberry people out there; we all know one another just by being in the business. I didn't know her well, though. Just enough to say hello."

"Do you have any theories, as to what may have happened to her?"

Elizabeth shook her head. "She had a reputation for being, I guess you'd call it wild. Her disappearance came as a shock, of course. Generally, people at the time—at least the people I talked to—seemed to think she had simply left her husband. I never thought so, though. She didn't seem the type. To just up and leave, I mean. She'd want a settlement. A big juicy divorce settlement. I always suspected foul play."

As the two women talked, Lena kept an eye on the vultures. They served as her barometer. When she saw a half dozen suddenly rise from the swamp to join their brethren in the air she surmised that the funeral entourage had finally reached its goal.

"Did you suspect anyone in particular?" Lena inquired.

Elizabeth shrugged. "Everyone seems to suspect the husband."

"Do you suspect him?"

"I don't know whom to suspect, or what to think. It came as a terrible shock—when I heard they'd found Amanda's remains. Like I say, I always felt that something bad must have happened to the poor girl."

She dabbed at her eyes—the tears being for Pal, Lena assumed, rather than for Amanda. Though the woman did seem genuinely tenderhearted, in a blubbery sort of way. Her sorrow might encompass all of the world's woes, the animal kingdom's as well as humanity's, for all Lena knew.

"Whatever her morals were like," Elizabeth added, "she didn't deserve something like this to happen to her. It's horrible to think of.

Her lying dead like that, all those years, under the vines."

With that she fell silent. Perhaps she was thinking of her four-footed Pal, who would likewise be lying dead, for years and years to come, under the sod, or however they interred dogs at Angel View. Odd name for a pet cemetery, Lena reflected. Did it imply that the deceased pets had a view of angels? Or was it the angels who had a view of the pets? And the angels themselves—who, or what, were they? Regular (that is to say, *people*) angels, or *animal* angels? Were the pets who were buried there now angels, in perpetual view of the humans who came to visit their graves? It was all very confusing.

As much as Lena loved Marmalade, she could not picture him as an angel, with a little golden halo hovering above his orange head, tilted to one side, and a pair of feathered wings sprouting from his back, a beatific smile on his whiskered face.

The two women sat, each lost in her own thoughts, Lena's—not uncharacteristically—verging on the outré, Elizabeth's—as betrayed by dismal sighs, leaky eyes and nostrils—decidedly morose.

Thoughts of angels led, progressively, to thoughts of saints. Her own sainthood, or entrée into heaven, should be guaranteed, Lena reflected, as just—though woefully inadequate—payment for the martyrdom she was suffering in having to endure, at close quarters, her companion's copious snorts and wheezes.

"It's a good thing Brian Siminski came along when he did," she said, in a further attempt to distract the woman from the morbid thoughts that were causing the leakage. "Your husband and sister would have a rough go of it without his help. You seemed to recognize him the other day. Has he done work for you?"

Elizabeth shook her head. "His brother worked for us one or two seasons."

"Oh, I didn't know he had a brother," Lena said. "He's a quiet young man and doesn't say much."

Elizabeth looked at her oddly. "His brother's dead. He was killed in that terrible accident."

"I'm sorry to hear that," Lena said. "Did the accident happen recently?"

"Why, no. Years ago. I'm surprised you don't remember." She

shrugged. "But then, there are so many accidents involving young people, how can anyone keep track of them all."

"So it was an automobile accident?"

Elizabeth nodded. "There was another boy killed, too. A bunch of them were in the car. Evidently they had been drinking. They were all under age."

"Was Brian one of them?"

"Yes. Though I don't think he was badly hurt."

They sat for a while in silence. Lena wondered whether trauma relating to his brother's death might account for Brian's almost pathologically shy nature.

"Odd, now that I think of it," Elizabeth mused. "The accident. It happened around the same time that Amanda Verfurth disappeared. That same night, if I recall. I remember the details, because like I said one of the boys—Brad, Brian's brother—had worked for us on the bogs one or two summers. Poor kid. He probably would have worked for us that year, too."

The emergence from the swamp of the "retrieval crew"—Lena could hardly think of them as a rescue team—brought to a close Elizabeth's somber recollections. The three had made of the tarpaulin a stretcher (catafalque or bier would be the more accurate term) upon which to transport the body through the dense brush. For sensibilities' sake—Elizabeth's especially—they had draped the bed sheet over the carcass. God only knew what condition the poor brute was in, having served as smorgasbord for a dozen vultures.

Would the folks at the pet cemetery prepare the body for viewing? Or would they recommend a closed casket?

Elizabeth left the cab to assist her husband and sister and their helper as, visibly exhausted, they approached the SUV. Brian led the way, holding up his end of the tarpaulin while walking backward; Marguerite and Harvey struggled along, leaning forward, each holding onto a corner at their end. The exposed flesh of all three bore scratch marks from briars and sharp branches, as well as welts from insect bites.

Well meaning but ineffectual, Elizabeth managed to get in their way. Harvey glared at his wife in exasperation as, impediment to their forward motion, she blundered from one point to another. Finally she stood aside, and they were able to slide the tarpaulin into the SUV. Was the situation emblematic, Lena wondered, of the woman's existence? Always an encumbrance, never a help?

With Pal securely tucked in, the three erstwhile pall bearers took a moment to regain an upright posture and catch their wind. They stood well apart from one another—as if, mission accomplished, they did not wish to be misconstrued as a close-knit team. Brian, in particular, held himself aloof—not, apparently, out of hostility, but as if abashed by his involvement.

It was Marguerite who, at last, took the initiative and broke the silence. Going up to Brian, she thanked him for his kind help and clasped his hand in hers. He seemed taken aback by the gesture, caught off guard, as if wondering what the fuss was all about, but managed, albeit awkwardly, to complete the handshake.

Harvey mumbled his thanks, too, as did Elizabeth. All three then thanked Lena for having located Pal in the first place, and for going to the trouble of showing them the way.

"Since you won't accept the thousand dollar reward, we'd like to donate it in your name to a charity of your choice," Harvey announced before climbing into the SUV.

Her first impulse was to decline even that. But she changed her mind, knowing that the Walderne-cum-Cardozo clan could well afford the sum, would in fact feel better if she acceded to their proposal.

"Well, if you insist..." She considered for a moment, then named The Wildlands Trust of Southeastern Massachusetts. After all, the turkey vultures had been denied their bounty. The least she could do was to help an organization that would work to preserve the birds' habitat.

As, kicking up dust, the SUV pulled away, Brian remained behind. Studying his van, Lena felt that it would have made the better hearse, black, compact, just the right size for the obsequies of a pampered pet.

"I've finished the pump house," Brian said.

"Already!" Lena exclaimed. "That was quick. Let's go have a look-see." The anticipated glass of wine...well, that could wait.

CHAPTER VIII

A Person of Interest

Ever since she'd hired a cranberry growers' service to relieve her of some of the more onerous responsibilities of bog ownership—frost protection, weed and pest control, dike maintenance, irrigation, harvesting—Lena found that she had a lot of free time on her hands. Not that she ever felt bored—her interests were far too varied for that to happen—but she did, from time to time, feel restless.

Fixing up the screenhouse, even though she would not be doing the work herself, seemed like a worthwhile project to keep her busy. The building was over a hundred years old; like many antiquated screenhouses it was in danger of falling into disrepair. These venerable edifices, indispensable to the cranberry industry in the nineteenth and early twentieth centuries, when growers harvested, stored, packed, and shipped their own crops—having first screened the berries, of course: rid them of loose vines and chaff, and picked out the rotten or unripe fruit—had become, by the latter half of the twentieth century, obsolete. Redundant, home to rats, bats, and owls, they were now used, if at all, for the storage of equipment.

The plight of screenhouses reminded Lena of the old barns that used to dot the New England countryside, so familiar to her childhood: quaint, picturesque, historic—and neglected, so much so that they had all but disappeared.

Lena's screenhouse was haunted. But Joe Baker, the resident ghost, would surely not object to a few necessary repairs; it was after all his home.

Who—besides herself, and possibly Cheryl—believed in ghosts anyhow?

⌒⌒

Brian put a damper on her plans.

As soon as the SUV with its nimbus of road dust had disappeared around the bend, Lena climbed into her pickup. Followed at a distance by Brian in his funereal van, she drove down to the pump house, where a quick inspection revealed that the young carpenter, as expected, had done a yeoman's job. The renovated building looked spanking new, sturdier than ever, ready for another twenty or thirty years of service. And, like a true professional, he had cleaned up after himself, leaving no split shingles or half-sawn boards, no sawdust or shavings, no stray nails to flatten tires.

"Do you believe in ghosts?" she asked as, ready to go their separate ways, they stood before their respective vehicles.

He raised an eyebrow; the question had obviously taken him by surprise. Still sweaty from his exertions in the swamp, he mopped at his forehead with a handkerchief before shrugging his shoulders and saying, "Not really." After a moment's reflection he added: "I don't think so."

She told him about *her* ghost, Joe Baker, a bog worker who decades ago drowned one frost night in an irrigation canal, but who occasionally was seen in her screenhouse warming himself by the old wood stove, or most often, was not seen—but who always left a little puddle of water where he had, supposedly, been sitting.

"I'm telling you about Joe Baker because the screenhouse is due for repairs, if you're interested."

He hesitated.

Why, Lena wondered, did she always get the feeling that this young man, in his quiet reserve, was hiding something—as if perpetually embarrassed, or ashamed, of…what? She couldn't pinpoint it. At first she had thought he was merely shy. But now she felt there was something beyond that. Could it be guilt at his brother's death? So-called "survivor's guilt," for having walked away from the accident unscathed?

"You're not afraid of the ghost?" she asked.

He smiled, a slight curl of the lips, an expression almost of sad wisdom, and shook his head. "I'd like to get going on your screenhouse, Mrs. Lombardi. But I can't right away. I got another job I gotta do first."

"Oh? So work is starting to come your way? I'm glad to hear that." She was tempted to add: "I'm not surprised. You're a conscientious worker." But that might cause him embarrassment. Instead she said, "My screenhouse can wait. When you finish with your current job please give me a call, or just stop by. You can check out the screenhouse then and give me your expert opinion on what needs doing."

He nodded but promised nothing.

A week went by, and then another, and still Lena did not hear from Brian. She could kick herself for not having asked how long this new job of his would take to complete. She hadn't even inquired as to who had hired him. It was not like her to be so tactful. But, she told herself, she had wanted to respect his reticence. She had, in fact, assumed that it was some minor job that would take but a few days.

She could always call his aunt. Phyllis would know how to reach him. But Lena had no cogent reason for doing so. As she herself had told him, the screenhouse could wait. In the meantime she turned her attention to other matters, in particular the unsolved murder of Amanda Verfurth.

From what she could gather from the media, there were two new developments in the case: the authorities had begun referring to Kurt Verfurth, the murdered woman's husband, as a "person of interest;" and a spokesperson for the police stated that an arrest was imminent. Putting the two together, things, in Lena's estimation, did not look good for Mr. Verfurth.

He was of course a logical, if not the prime, suspect.

Surely he had a plausible motive for wanting his wife out of the way: her philandering. He might have killed her in a jealous rage. Or more damning, with premeditation—if she were threatening divorce, one which would bring a hefty settlement for herself. Or he might have done her in as punishment for infidelity. Second, he had opportunity, in abundance. His alibi, it turned out, was no alibi at all. True, at the time of Amanda's disappearance witnesses claimed to have seen him in Yarmouth Port, caring for his father. So what? He could have snuck away from the old gent at any time during the night, returned home, dispatched Amanda to the nether world (or wherever the souls of such creatures go), disposed of her body, and returned to his mentally impaired, indeed semi-vegetative, parent, with no one the wiser. Third, his wife's body, what was left of it, was found tucked beneath the vines of *his* cranberry bog.

Those were the circumstances—you could hardly call them pieces of evidence—against Kurt Verfurth.

In his favor was the fact that he had, in the ten years since Amanda's disappearance, led an exemplary, an apparently blameless—some might even say reclusive—life. He had worked hard raising cranberries, and kept largely to himself. But was that surprising, in view of the fact that many folks in the area, including neighbors and former friends, presuming his guilt, shunned him, openly or otherwise?

There was one other factor which, if viewed objectively, might cause some to doubt Kurt Verfurth's guilt: his decision to have the vines on that remote section of bog stripped and replanted with a more productive variety. Would a murderer, having successfully concealed his victim's body for nearly a decade, make such a decision? It was difficult to imagine such hubris, even on the part of the most reckless of criminals.

Or had stripping the vines been a calculated risk, a clever ploy? If Kurt was the murderer, if he had killed his wife and secreted her body under the vines, he had lived with that dark secret for nearly a decade. Ten long years of self-recrimination and sleepless nights. How, assuming he was an imaginative man, not entirely devoid of conscience, the guilty knowledge must have weighed—nay, preyed—upon his mind! How must the ghost of Amanda—if only her image, if only the memory of her—have haunted his dreams! What if her remains were unearthed? What if, on their own accord, they rose unhallowed from the makeshift grave to seek revenge?

Nonsense, of course. But a guilty mind...

To ease the pressure...

Why *not* have the bog stripped and the vines replanted with a more productive variety? There was a good chance that the remains would not be discovered, that they would be rolled up with the turf, carted to shore unseen, to compost in a heap of vegetative debris off to one side.

No matter. Let the bones arise, let them see the light of day. Would the perpetrator of a heinous crime make such a decision? Would a fiendish murderer take such a risk? Of course not! Kurt Verfurth must be an innocent man.

Or so he may have, deviously, reasoned.

CHAPTER IX
The Diary…continued

Dear Diary:

Funny how things work out. The best laid schemes…

You see, it was never my intention, ten years ago, to kill the bitch Amanda. To frighten her, yes. To threaten her with bodily harm, admittedly. But to actually bring about her death? No. At least I don't think so. I have, of course, over the past decade given the matter much thought.

It could have been, I suppose, a subconscious desire on my part to…how shall I put it…rid the world of a pest. For that's what Amanda Verfurth was. A pest.

At least to me she was.

A pest and a threat.

So it is conceivable that I set out that evening fully intending—at a subconscious level, you understand—to strike the fatal blow that caused her to lose her balance, fall, and hit her head against the stone wall.

There! I have said it!

So much for withholding secrets! Despite my resolve never to confide in you, I find that I must share my innermost thoughts with someone, some thing. I am, after all, only human. Am I not? Am I not human?

My mistrust of your infallibility (your ability to remain hidden from prying eyes) is overshadowed by my need to...

What?

Ask forgiveness? Absurd! I feel no guilt. No sense of wrongdoing.

I feel no sorrow.

No pity.

No remorse.

For what I have done I feel no shame.

I feel...nothing.

My need is far greater than merely to feel.

My need is to exult.

My need is to shout out to the world: "It was I who killed the skulking bitch!"

CHAPTER X
The Dancing Picaroon

Even before the rain became heavy Cheryl and Lena lost electric power—a downed line, presumably, a not uncommon occurrence, what with all the overhanging branches on the back roads, and the wind gusting at forty miles an hour. Although it was midday, the murk brought in by the storm made it seem like early evening.

"'The rain is a writer / dotting its i's against the window pane / crossing its t's with thunder.' Funny how I can remember the words, but not the name of the poet. No one famous, I'm sure."

The two women were seated in the library, sipping red wine in front of a brisk fire, listening to the wind-driven rain strike against the house, amidst flashes of lightning and the fierce rumble of thunder. Marmalade, for reasons known only to himself, had forsaken his customary position before the hearth to lie sprawled on a scatter rug in a far corner of the room.

"He probably can't fathom why we've lit a fire this close to the Fourth of July," Lena said, in an attempt to explain the cat's unwonted behavior.

"Maybe he just finds it too hot," Cheryl ventured.

"That's possible," Lena conceded. "Do you have any plans for the Fourth?" she asked, after they had sat silent for a while.

"Anthony and I may spend some time in Newport," Cheryl said. "Friends of his have offered the use of their condo while they're away. How about joining us? We'd love to have you, Lena. I know you don't like to leave Marmalade for any length of time, but it would only be for two or three days."

"It's kind of you to invite me, dear, but I've seen enough Newport mansions to last me a lifetime. As soon as this weather clears— it's beginning to sound like the Fourth already, did you hear that boom!—I'd like to get going on the repairs to the screenhouse. That is, if I can get hold of Brian."

"Oh, I meant to tell you," Cheryl said. "I saw your itinerant carpenter this morning."

"So he hasn't fallen off the face of the earth after all," Lena remarked. "I was beginning to wonder about that young man. Where ever did you see him?"

"At Wareham Crossing as I was leaving Target."

"Did you talk to him?"

Cheryl shook her head. "He was with two other men. At least I assume the three of them were together. They seemed to be having some sort of argument."

"With whom?" Lena asked.

"With each other," Cheryl replied.

"What about?"

"Now Lena, how would I know? It had already started to rain and I was hurrying directly to my car. They were standing in the parking lot a few car lengths away. I got the impression they were having some sort of verbal disagreement, that's all."

Lena reached for the nearly empty bottle of Pinot Noir that stood on a small table beside her and coaxed the few remaining drops into her glass. "A heated argument?"

"I don't know," Cheryl said. "I got the impression that one of the men was very angry with Brian and the third fellow. The strange thing is, they were speaking very softly, as if afraid of being overheard."

"So you couldn't hear what they were saying?" Lena asked.

"No. The only reason I noticed them in the first place was because one of the men was—well, rather conspicuous."

"Good looking?" Lena inquired.

Cheryl laughed. "Only if you find pirates irresistible."

"Pirates? What have they got to do with any of this?" Lena cast a suspicious glance at Cheryl's half-empty glass. "The wine hasn't gone to your head, has it dear? I don't see how it can have, since I've been hogging most of it."

"That you have indeed," Cheryl said amiably. "But to answer your question: the young man I'm referring to was conspicuous because he wore a black patch over one eye. And his face, at least from a distance, looked badly scarred."

"Ah. Like a buccaneer," Lena said. "Disfigured from all those knockdown sword fights they get into on the high seas. Or by flying splinters from timbers shattered by cannon balls. Was the pirate the one who acted angry? Brian seems so quiet; I can't imagine anyone, even a hardened swashbuckler, getting upset with him. But pirates do have a reputation for being evil-tempered."

"Lena! Don't be absurd. I only meant to say that, because of the eye patch, the young man called to mind a pirate." Cheryl shook her head in mock chagrin. "Actually, it was the third fellow who seemed upset with both Brian and the one wearing the patch." She picked up her glass and took a hefty swallow. "Let's not make a mountain out of a molehill. You could hardly categorize their disagreement as a barroom brawl, or even a quarrel. It just struck me as strange, that's all: the way they were standing there, oblivious, or at least indifferent, to the rain."

A flash of lightning, so close to where the women were sitting, they could hear the crackle, followed in a split second by a thunderclap that shook the window panes, sent Marmalade scurrying off the scatter rug, across the room, and beneath the sofa.

It was another three hours before power was restored; by then the two women had consumed a second bottle of wine, and night had fallen in earnest. They had a late supper, leftovers heated in the microwave, and turned in early. Lena had trouble falling asleep—the wine; too much affected her that way—and when she did achieve a fitful slumber, she dreamt of piracy on the high seas.

She waited until after the holiday to phone Phyllis.

"I have more work for your nephew but have no idea how to

contact him," she explained. "Whenever I brought up the subject of an address he became vague, almost evasive, as if he didn't want me to know his whereabouts or even his phone number. I don't even know what town he lives in."

"He's been staying with friends, here and there," Phyllis said. "The last I knew he was holed up somewhere in South Carver. He stops by to visit me at least once a week but he never says much about his personal life." She paused. "I invited him over for the Fourth but he didn't show up. He's like that: moody. He doesn't get along with his parents—my brother and his wife; I'm the only real family he has except for them. Now that he's on his feet again—I mean, working regularly—I'm in hopes that he'll settle down. You know, find a permanent place to stay, even if its only a small studio apartment."

"Do you happen to know if he's on a job now?" Lena asked.

"The last I knew he was doing odd jobs for Harvey Cardozo."

Harvey Cardozo? How odd.

Harvey must have hired Brian when they went into the swamp to fetch Pal's body, Lena theorized. Was that Harvey's way of repaying the young man for helping to carry out the dead dog?

"Well, the next time you see Brian, please ask him to get in touch with me," Lena said.

Although they arrived on her property at irregular intervals, depending on what jobs needed doing, crews from the cranberry growers' service kept Lena's bog in tiptop shape. Occasionally, during their lunch break, she would bring the workers pies or cakes fresh from her oven. Baking gave her something to do, and she enjoyed her brief chats with the workers, who appreciated the homemade treats she provided and didn't seem to mind her eccentricities, one of which was to pitch in on a whim and help with whatever task they were performing.

A practice—one could hardly call it an eccentricity; perhaps a peculiarity?—of hers which some of the workers viewed with amusement, others with dismay, was taking potshots at muskrats with a .22

(sometimes her pistol, more often her rifle). Lena was a crack shot and seldom missed; one day she bagged two of the pesky rodents.

"They're actually a large vole," she explained to Cheryl, who deplored the killing of wildlife. "I don't need to tell you how destructive they can be, with their constant tunneling. Besides, their bodies are not wasted."

"Whatever do you mean?" Cheryl asked, appalled—mindful of the Canada geese Lena would now and then bring to the table, and worse, the slimy eels she would skin, cut up and fry, still squirming, in those formidable cast iron pans she'd purchased at auction.

"I don't skin and eat the muskrats, dear, if that's what you're thinking," Lena reassured her. "I've eaten possum, of course, and raccoon, and even skunk, but I draw the line at muskrat. I leave the bodies out for the vultures, as recompense for the role I played in depriving them of Pal's carcass."

Feigning to misinterpret the look of incredulity which Cheryl directed toward her, she hastily added: "Well, they would hardly do as a meal for Marmalade, would they? They're much too cumbersome for his small teeth, not to mention the toughness of their hide."

Although there was no real work for her to do around the bog, Lena had, to occupy her time, her house, her cat, her garden, her friendship with Cheryl, her little confrontations with destructive critters, not to mention books and the appreciation of fine wines. Such was the quietude, the serenity of her days.

If evil impended, she was not aware of it.

Early one morning in mid July Brian Siminski showed up at her door.

Though the young man was clean-shaven and neatly dressed, and bronzed from working outdoors, something about his appearance disturbed her. There was a gaunt look to his eyes—the haunted look of someone who for weeks running has spent sleepless nights. He had lost weight, a considerable amount, or so it seemed to her. But there was something beyond that...

Lena greeted him warmly, and with motherly concern (he had grown too thin!) invited him in for coffee and cranberry muffins. "I baked them yesterday," she told him, "with frozen berries from last year's crop."

He shook his head politely. "I just had breakfast." He stepped back from the threshold. "I'm ready to look at your screenhouse, Mrs. Lombardi, if this is a good time."

"As good a time as any."

She stepped onto the portico, locking the door behind her. It was only then that she noticed Brian's van parked in the drive, and a figure in the passenger seat: a young man with a badly scarred face, and a black eye patch over his left eye.

The pirate!

The man with the eye patch politely got out of the van so that Lena could sit in front. He was shorter than Brian, and thin—wiry, as if, she imagined, he could twist himself into knots—with blond hair cropped almost to his scalp. Not the hairdo of your typical pirate! Though surely some of those old-time picaroons had fair hair and wore it short, Lena supposed. They would have wrapped a kerchief or bandanna around their head in lieu of a hat. If not for the scars he might have been quite handsome—not just the scars, but also the eye patch, and a certain vacancy in his eyes, as if a part of him, a portion of his mind, was on permanent leave of absence.

Brian introduced him. "This is Eric."

Eric smiled, revealing a missing front tooth. Lena smiled back, trying not to stare at his face.

She climbed into the passenger seat. Eric closed the door for her before getting into the back.

Eric, it turned out, was Brian's helper.

He spoke little—less than Brian, if that were possible. When he did say something, the words came out slowly, almost haltingly, as when inspecting the screenhouse Brian—out of kindness, it seemed, rather than necessity—asked him his opinion concerning the condition of certain clapboards. Assessing the missing left eye, and the hideously scarred face, Lena surmised that, as a result of whatever calamity befell him, Eric had suffered serious brain trauma.

She recalled the "terrible accident" Elizabeth Walderne had mentioned, in which Brian's brother and another boy had been killed. There had been other teenagers involved, who like Brian had survived. Could Eric be one of them?

"Is it as dilapidated as it looks?" Lena asked when, having spent a good half hour eye-balling and poking around, Brian was ready to give his assessment.

He shook his head. "The building's more or less sound. The roof needs patching; you can see places where the shingles have come loose." He kicked a fallen asphalt shingle with his foot, and pointed to an area on the peak surrounding the weathercock. "You've got some rotten clapboards," he went on, "especially on the north-facing side; they hafta be replaced. Some of the windows, too, though that could run into money."

"We'll take care of the roof and clapboards first," Lena said. "Then we'll think about the windows."

"You might get by a few more years with just a little caulking," Brian suggested. "It's not like you're looking to make the building energy-efficient."

"Is that all?" Lena asked, pleased that she would not be facing any major expenditures.

"There's signs of powder post beetles inside, in the rough boards on the partition between the room with the wood stove and the bigger area."

"Oh, dear!" Lena exclaimed. "A serious infestation?"

"Naw. Just some little piles of sawdust here and there. I'd hafta replace a couple boards, that's all, and spray the rest with insecticide. A can of Raid will do the trick."

"Can I spray 'em?" Eric interjected. "I like killing bugs!" His one good eye beamed; as if unable to contain his excitement he danced around on one leg, while holding the other out at an angle as if it were a peg of wood.

Lena glanced at the young man askance. An image conjured itself up, of Eric, kerchief knotted around his head, a gold earring dangling from one lobe, wielding a pistol in one hand and a cutlass in the other, hacking away at giant cockroaches as they swarmed up the sides of his ship. Or Eric, with an actual pegleg, seated on a keg of rum unscrewing the leg and spraying it with Raid to kill the powder post beetles.

As apology for his friend's outburst, Brian offered Lena a wan smile. To Eric he said: "You can spray the beetles, old buddy, if you want to. I promise. I'll tell you when, though, okay?"

CHAPTER XI
...continued

Dear Diary:

I've been thinking...

All along what a fool I've been! It should have been apparent to me from the very outset: The discovery of Amanda's bones changes everything. Everything. You do see that, don't you? You do get my drift?

Those others...Those meddlers...

Were it not for them...

It does not take an Einstein to see that further steps are necessary.

The time to act is now.

CHAPTER XII
Footfalls

Eric Russel sat on the ground by the edge of the swamp in the shade of a lofty pine, munching at a peanut butter and jelly sandwich between sips from a can of cranberry-flavored soda. The peanut butter was salted and crunchy, his favorite kind. The jelly was grape. You wouldn't think that grape and cranberry would go good together, but they did, if one was jelly and the other soda. His mom had made the sandwich fresh that morning. Whenever he was on a job she always gave him peanut butter and jelly, though not always grape. Sometimes it was strawberry, or maybe raspberry. The bread was always whole wheat. Eric preferred plain white bread but his mom said whole wheat was better for him. He always listened to his mom and tried to follow her advice.

His mom was good to him. She always took care to write his name in ink on the brown paper bag she packed his lunch in—as if there could ever be any confusion as to which bag belonged to him! Brian was good to him, too. Brian was his best friend. Brian always gave him work, whenever there was any to give. In the fall, during the cranberry harvest season, Eric could easily find work. Bog owners were always looking for people to help harvest the crop. But the rest of the year was different. Jobs were hard to come by for someone like him, who had no skills, to speak of.

He liked working with Brian. Brian was patient with him. Brian understood that sometimes he was a little slow to learn, especially if it was something complicated, like measuring exactly where to cut a board, or where to drill a hole. He liked working for Mrs. Lombardi, too. She was a nice old lady. She baked things for him and Brian. Pies and muffins and cakes and cookies. Eric's mom was a good cook, but she didn't have time to bake. She worked two jobs. Eric felt bad that he couldn't earn enough money to help his mom out more. He brightened, though, at the thought that at the end of this week he would have a paycheck to give to her.

He peeked into his lunch bag. For dessert his mom had given him a bright green apple. He decided to leave it there for now. Just in case Mrs. Lombardi came by with something good. He could always eat the apple later, if she didn't come by.

It was hot, even in the shade. His head felt cloudy. Maybe he could take a quick nap. Brian wouldn't mind. In fact, Brian had made him promise not to go back to work until Brian returned from his errand. Eric grinned to himself. Today was the day to tackle the powder post beetles. He still felt a little sheepish, for having made a spectacle of himself last week in front of Mrs. Lombardi. What must she think of him? He was only joking about liking to kill bugs—though there was some truth to the statement. Anyhow, today was the day. Brian had forgotten to bring the bug spray along, and had gone to the store at lunch time to fetch it.

He would not be back for another fifteen or twenty minutes. In the meantime, Eric would snooze.

He had hardly fallen asleep, though, when he awoke to the sound of someone approaching on foot. Not Brian, surely. He hadn't heard his van arrive. Mrs. Lombardi, perhaps. With something good for him to eat. Funny, though, he hadn't heard her pickup—or sometimes she came in her sedan—either. He opened his eye—he had only the one—to see who it might be.

Lying there, in the full dazzle of the midday sun, he could hear the footfalls heading toward him, approaching from his blind side. When he stood up and turned, he was surprised to see that it was neither Brian nor Mrs. Lombardi coming near. He knew who it was, though, and smiled.

CHAPTER XIII
In the Shadows

Brian Siminski watched as black heat waves, like mirages of last spring's puddles, shimmered in pools above the asphalt. The rays of the sun glinted off the mirrors of parked cars like a furtive message sent in code. Staring through the windshield in the bright light made his eyes tired. He should wear shades in the summer, but never bothered to.

He reached behind the seat, pulled out a plastic bottle of tepid tap water, and took a deep swig. The water was warm, but at least it was wet.

WBZ was a good radio station by which to check the time. He switched on the ignition, and drumming his fingers against the rim of the steering wheel, listened impatiently through two commercial messages. Finally the announcer said: "One ten."

So, he had been sitting there, in the hot sun, with hardly a breeze—despite the wide-open windows the air stifling, hardly breathable—for more than half an hour. Obviously Jay had stood him up. And with Jay's refusal to give out his cell phone number, he had no means of communication.

In exasperation Brian slammed his fist against the wheel; mouthing expletives he shifted into gear and pulled out of the parking lot. Despite his anger, he as always drove cautiously, defensively. More so than usual, because his hands were shaking so.

Brian was more than just annoyed; he was pissed. It was Jay who had insisted on the impromptu meeting. It couldn't wait, he had said over the phone. (It was okay for Jay to phone *him*.) And of course it was not a subject they could discuss by e-mail or otherwise than in person. Nothing they could put in writing, in any form, or risk having someone secretly record.

Brian was sick of it. He wanted out. Had from the very beginning.

But how?

⸙

Eric would be wondering what was keeping him.

Brian felt guilty, lying to his friend, pretending to have forgotten the can of Raid. It had been a simple subterfuge, one that only someone like Eric would fall for. That's what made it so shameful, his taking advantage of his friend's gullibility. But of course there was no real harm in it. The opposite, actually. Eric got to enjoy a longer lunch hour, that's all.

What was Jay up to this time? What was he thinking?

Well, Brian really didn't give a sweet shit what Jay had in mind, or the reason behind the sudden urgency. He, Brian, had made up his mind. For once he would do the right thing. Regardless of the consequences.

He just had to work out the details.

His mind was still a jumble of conflicting thoughts when he swung onto the circular drive that led by the old lady's house onto the dirt road which, skirting the bog, led eventually to the screenhouse. Both her vehicles, the battered-up Ford pickup and the slightly more respectable sedan, were parked there. Her cat, the fat orange tabby, was asleep on the grass, in the shade of a huge white oak.

Mrs. Lombardi and her cat!

It was comical, to a young man like Brian, the way she doted on the creature. If Brian were offered the choice to lead a life other than his own, he would choose to be Mrs. Lombardi's cat. The old lady was dotty, no doubt about it. Even so he admitted to liking—and respecting—her. She was generous; she paid well, and on time. And she had a kind heart. She was very intelligent, too, if you overlooked her peculiarities. She knew just about all there was to know about

77

cranberries, and understood quite a bit about other things too, like carpentry and engineering.

Most important of all, she tolerated Eric.

Brian's van sent up a cloud of dust as he sped (faster than usual) over the parched dirt track. He was in a hurry to get back to the screenhouse. Not that he didn't trust Eric to keep out of trouble, but still…Eric was Eric.

He drew up to the clearing and selected a shady spot in which to park, under the drooping boughs of a tall pine by the side of the building. He got out of the vehicle and stretched his legs. He looked for Eric, but his friend was nowhere in sight.

Eric's absence was no cause for concern, of course. He could be anywhere: inside the screenhouse (though it would be hot and stuffy in there, what with the dead air afloat with dust motes), or behind it, stretched out on the bare ground, fast asleep. (Eric seemed to require an awful lot of sleep—something to do with his injuries?) Or he may have grown restless waiting for Brian and gone for a walk.

He wouldn't go far. (One thing about Eric, he knew his own limitations. He would be too afraid of getting lost.)

He wouldn't have climbed onto the staging that Brian had set up on the north side of the building in order to replace the rotting clap-boards. He had strict orders never to set foot on the staging, or even a ladder, unless Brian was there with him. Eric would not dare to even think of disregarding such orders, of that Brian was confident. Even so, on his way to check the rear of the screenhouse he went by the north side, just in case, and glanced upward.

Nothing there, as expected.

Nor as Brian rounded the building did he find Eric stretched out behind it asleep in the shade.

Maybe he had gone into the swamp to relieve himself.

"Eric?" he called out, loudly.

No reply.

He called again. The stillness, the unanswering silence, was palpable.

Okay. Two possibilities. Either Eric was inside the building, not responding to Brian's shouted summons for whatever reason—probably because, dozing in a chair (or even curled up on the floor), he was lost in dreamland. Or he had gone for a walk and had not yet returned—possibly because, easily disoriented, he had lost his way.

But in the latter instance wouldn't Brian, on his way in, have spotted his friend?

Not necessarily. He had not been looking for Eric. And Eric might simply have been out of sight: behind a tree, or around a bend. In the sand pit. Anywhere.

He'd just have to go looking for him.

Brian wasn't at all worried. Why should he be? Eric was an adult—twenty-seven years old—even if he was, just the slightest bit, impaired. He most definitely was not what you would call retarded. Just slow. (All because of damage to his brain from the accident.) And not all that slow—once something imprinted itself in his mind, no matter how complex, it tended to stay there. His memory wasn't bad in itself—except for the amnesia. Eric could remember nothing about the accident, and very little of his life before it. But he was by no means simple-minded.

He just needed looking after.

So, tired of waiting for Brian to return from his fool's errand, he had in all likelihood gone off for a stroll. He couldn't have wandered too far, especially in this heat. Brian chuckled to himself. Eric had probably meandered a half mile or so, along the perimeter of the bog or down one of the old side trails, then, feeling drowsy, had sat down to rest a minute or two, and promptly fallen asleep. He'd be all apologetic when, finally, Brian located him.

Which shouldn't take too long to do.

First, though, it made sense for Brian to check inside the screen-house.

The side door of the old building was propped open with a two-by-four, just as he had left it that morning after replacing the bee-tle-damaged boards on the interior partition. He had purposely left the door open so that the place would air out before they came back to treat the remaining boards with insect spray.

He poked his head into the anteroom and shouted: "Eric?"

The result was a hollow echo, his voice reverberating between the uninsulated walls, mocking the futility of the endeavor. Well, he hadn't really expected Eric to answer; he doubted whether his friend was anywhere near the screenhouse. But he stepped inside anyhow, into the little room where, according to Mrs. Lombardi, the old-time growers used to gather on frost nights to sit by the wood stove and keep one another company. She had even bragged to him that the building was haunted by the ghost of one of the men—a man named Joe Baker—who had drowned one frost night after falling into his own irrigation canal.

The room felt gloomy enough to be haunted. What little light there was came filtered through dusty window panes smeared with fly specks and draped with cobwebs. An ancient wood stove—quite possibly the original from a century and a half ago—stood off to one side, a half dozen mismatched chairs arranged in a semicircle before it, waiting for the old-timers to stop by and sit, coffee mugs in hand, and warm their toes by the fire. Like a relic from the days of tall ships, an old lacquered sea chest sat in one corner. It, too, was covered in dust. Earlier, he had been tempted to lift the lid and rummage through it—what treasures might it contain!—but of course, out of scruples, he hadn't.

No sign of Eric here. Nor was he likely to be in the next room, the main area of the screenhouse from which the anteroom had been partitioned off.

He'd take a look anyhow. He crossed the room to the inner door, and was about to yank it open, when he noticed something odd. The floor boards, which just before lunch Eric had swept free of sawdust and shavings from the morning's repair work, showed signs of dampness. Not the puddle of water which Joe Baker's ghost was said to leave behind. Just a wet spot, about the size of a half dollar.

Brian retraced his steps to the outer door, and saw what, because of the poor light—and the fact that he hadn't been looking down—he'd failed to discern when he first entered the room: here and there just the faintest traces of dampness, scarcely visible, in a line and spaced apart as if left by wet shoes or boots. The marks were much too faint to determine what sort or size of boot might have left them. So faint, in fact, he would never have spied them if not for the damp spot by the threshold of the inner door—as if someone whose shoes were wet had paused there for a brief moment.

"Eric! You in there?"

The only scenario that made sense to any of this (supposing you didn't believe in ghosts) was if Eric had gone for a walk, had somehow taken a spill into a body of water—the shore ditch that ran the circumference of the bog?—and, dripping wet, had come back to the screenhouse. But for what purpose? Surely not to dry himself off? He could more readily do that out in the open, in the fresh air and under the sun.

Of course, there was no way of telling whether the wet footprints—if such they were—led in, or out. Perhaps Eric had contrived to step in some sort of liquid while inside the other room, and left the marks on his way out. Brian brought up a mental picture of the room—he'd been in it just a couple of hours earlier, while working on the partition—but couldn't remember seeing any containers that might have held water or anything similar.

It *was* water. But just to make sure…with his finger he touched one of the marks and brought the tip up close to his nostrils. The substance had no discernible smell—it wasn't gasoline—and didn't feel viscous, the way oil—or blood—might.

All of these thoughts ran through Brian's mind as he recrossed the room, took hold of the knob to the inner door, and pulled it open. He was wasting his time—if Eric was within hearing distance he would have replied to Brian's shout. Regardless, something seemed wrong; he might as well get to the bottom of it now.

He stepped into the darkened room. Heavy equipment (a tractor, a front-end loader, an old jalopy) and stacks of empty wooden cranberry boxes blocked many of the windows, so that little light penetrated. The unventilated air, in the July heat, felt oppressive, tainted with the stale fumes of gasoline and spilled motor oil. He paused. What, exactly, did he expect to find? Nothing, really. He glanced down at the floor, which in this portion of the building was of concrete, and saw what looked like drops of water. He looked up toward the roof—and immediately felt like a fool. Yeah, sure, a leak—when it hadn't rained in days.

Besides, if there was a leak in the roof he would have noticed the dampness on the floor that morning. But he hadn't, had he?

Well, of one thing he could be sure: he wouldn't find Eric anywhere in here.

He turned to leave. As he did so he caught, from the corner of his eye, what might be—but probably wasn't—movement. There, in the shadows behind the tractor, where a row of antiquated tools—pitch forks, sickles, scythes, pruning rakes—leaned against the wall.

In a vain attempt to penetrate the veil of blackness that obscured the area he leaned forward, and straining his eyes, peered into the dark. Without the aid of a flashlight he could make out any number of misshapen objects—which on closer inspection would prove to be everyday items used, or formerly used, around the bogs.

He shrugged. So now he was seeing things.

Again he turned to leave.

This time there could be no doubt. Something within the shadows moved.

He hesitated. He was as brave as the next guy, but this place was giving him the creeps. Blame it on Mrs. Lombardi's resident ghost, or just the circumstance of being alone in a deserted building. The prudent thing would be to leave at once. Outside, in the light of day, he could have a good laugh at himself, and then set about looking for Eric. If, that is, his friend wasn't already out there waiting for him by the van.

He wouldn't run, though. He wouldn't give way to panic. He would leave the building at his own reasoned pace: one step across the threshold and a slow stroll through the anteroom.

This time when Brian turned to leave he not only saw, he also heard, something. This time rather than mere shadow it was form that he saw, though indistinct. It was—also indistinct—a sort of scuffling that he heard. Boot leather against concrete?

This time whatever lurked in the shadows had not gone undetected.

It was too late, though. Brian had let down his guard. The form that like a frenzied dervish sprang forth from the shadows wielded a weapon, a blunt object, which crushed into his forehead and sent him sprawling onto the concrete floor. Stunned into semiconsciousness, he tried to raise himself; he lifted an arm to ward off the second blow. But it was no use. The object, a crowbar, smashed his elbow, and then his skull.

CHAPTER XIV
Angel Wings

"How is your research coming along, dear?" Lena asked her friend Cheryl.

The two women, as often was their wont, were sitting out the afternoon heat in the comfort of the screened-in gazebo that overlooked that portion of Lena's cranberry bog which lay directly behind her house. On the low metal table between them, a pitcher of ice-cold lemonade occupied the place of honor normally held by a bottle of chilled white wine; the substitution, unprecedented, was a consequence of Cheryl's suggestion that the older woman "lay off the stuff" for a bit.

"For harmony's sake I will kowtow to your demands," Lena averred, when pressed by Cheryl. "But on just this one occasion. My kowtowment, you understand, is but temporary."

"A temporary abstinence is better than none," Cheryl observed.

"What, after all, is a day without wine?" Lena countered. "What harm can there be in one or two glasses of what is, essentially, fruit juice? Think of the health benefits! The antioxidants!"

"Think of the damage to one's liver," Cheryl murmured, though she was secretly happy with her victory, however temporary.

Not everything in Lena's world was topsy-turvy. Wine might be denied her, but Marmalade lay in his customary spot, snoozing at her feet, an occasional switch of his tail the sole betrayal of some trifling annoyance, an itch perhaps, or the heat.

"My research? Not as well as I'd hoped," Cheryl said in reply to her friend's query. "I'm finding very little that I can actually describe as *folklore* pertaining to cranberries."

"Why do you suppose that is?" Lena asked. "I would think there'd be a wealth of material. As you know firsthand"—she gave her friend a meaningful look—"bogs can be mysterious places. Especially at night."

She reached for her glass—forgetting that it contained lemonade rather than Chardonnay. She remembered the substitution when her fingers were just shy of the stem; with a sigh that only unrequited love in the very young could otherwise call forth she let her hand fall limp onto the table.

"I've come to the conclusion that the cranberry industry began too late—in the first half of the nineteenth century—for any folkloric traditions to evolve," Cheryl said. "By that time most people had at least an elementary education. They no longer believed in witchcraft, pacts with the devil, magic potions, that sort of thing." She sighed. "As far as cranberries are concerned, I'm afraid that science got in the way of folklore."

"People still believe in ghosts," Lena said, by way of encouragement.

"That's true," Cheryl conceded. "Maybe I can come up with enough hauntings on or around the bogs to fill a book."

The women fell silent. They read for a while, Lena a tepid "thriller" borrowed from the town library—*real-life mysteries are far more fascinating than this fluff,* she grumbled to herself, as on the verge of drowsing she struggled to keep awake—Cheryl an antiquarian volume she'd stumbled upon at a used bookstore on Cape Cod. *What They Say in New England: A Book of Signs, Sayings, and Superstitions,* written by Clifton Johnson and published in 1896, was delightful and informative. Who would have guessed that people once believed that "If you have lost your cow" all you had to do was to "catch a grandpa-long-legs, put a finger on one leg, and he will point with another leg in the direction in which you will find the stray cow." Sadly, though, the book contained not a single mention of cranberries.

As for Lena…after five or six chapters of vapid prose in which, when the wooden characters were not busy killing one another in innovative, often hideous ways, they were busy having sex with one another in equally innovative, if not hideous, certainly grotesque, ways, she gave up. Tossing the offending book onto the table next to the lemonade—none too gently—she declared: "What that lemonade is to wine, this trash is to literature."

By way of reply Cheryl quoted: "'Carry a horse-chestnut in your pocket and you will not be troubled by rheumatism.'"

"Is that what your book says?" Lena asked. "It's a shame that there are no longer horse-chestnuts growing wild everywhere. I could use a nut or two, especially in damp weather. Alas, they've gone the way of the elms. Trees our grandparents knew, but which to us are lost to disease and blight."

"*Your* grandparents, perhaps," Cheryl said. "I'm not so sure about mine. What kind of chestnuts, I wonder, do they have in Portugal?"

"I was speaking of Americans collectively, dear." She glanced at her watch. "Goodness, it's already a quarter past five. I haven't seen the boys drive by, have you? They must be working late."

"Finishing up a project, no doubt," Cheryl said. She began to gather up the pitcher and glasses. "What time would you like supper?"

Lena reflected a moment. "In an hour or so? Around six-thirty? I'd like to drive down to the screenhouse first and see how things are going."

The temperature inside the pickup, hot enough to bake bread, gave Lena a wicked thirst. As she rolled down the windows before starting the engine perspiration began to bead on her forehead; by the time she got to the screenhouse (having en route breathed in the proverbial peck of dust which old-timers used to say each of us is destined to eat before we die) she longed for a glass or two of the ice-cold lemonade she had so readily disparaged, maybe the whole pitcher.

By now the boys, too, would have worked up a gargantuan thirst. Maybe she could induce them to stop by the house for something cold to drink before heading home, though she doubted it; the hour was getting late. They'd been on the job since before seven and were probably eager to get on home.

Or to the nearest bar.

That's where Lena would head, if she were a decade or two younger.

But did Brian drink? Perhaps not. And Eric? She doubted that, too. Despite his outré appearance he seemed more the sarsaparilla type.

Brian's van was parked by the side of the screenhouse, under the boughs of a tall pine at the edge of the swamp. She pulled up next to it. As she climbed out of the pickup she expected to hear the sounds of hammering or sawing, or the boys talking to one another.

Instead, silence greeted her.

Well, other than ordinary noises made by Brian and his one-eyed comrade plying their trade, what sounds did she expect to hear so late in the afternoon in mid July? Song birds at this hour were quiescent, except perhaps for the melodious trilling of hermit thrushes. It was a little early for birds to commence their evening search for food. The more obstreperous species, jays and crows, tended to be quiet, too, at this time. Even the Canada geese she'd passed on the way had been hunkered down in the heat on one of the dikes that bisected the bog.

She scanned the sky for hawks. Nothing in sight. Just a vulture or two floating high overhead as if on waves of heat, hoping for another Pal perhaps. And the sun, like a smashed yolk, leering down, on its slow westward slide.

Something didn't feel right. It was *too* quiet.

The side door to the screenhouse was propped open. Brian and Eric might be inside, though she doubted it, in this heat. Maybe they were taking a breather somewhere in the shade, prefatory to gathering up their tools. She doubted that too.

She stuck her head through the doorway. The anteroom was deserted, the inner door shut tight. They would not, in this dead air, be beyond, in the main portion of the screenhouse.

She went around to the north side. The scaffolding was still in place, and under it a figure she recognized as Brian's, sprawled on the ground face down, his arms stretched outward like a child making angel wings in the snow. Even from a distance of thirty feet it was obvious that he was badly hurt: unconscious, or dead. The shock of seeing the young man she had grown so fond of lying there inert, like a limp rag, took away, momentarily, Lena's powers to think, or to move.

When she did set herself in motion it was to act quickly. Rushing to the prostrate form she bent to feel his pulse. She could detect no signs of life, not the faintest heartbeat nor hint of breathing; at first she drew a glimmer of hope from the fact that his flesh felt warm to the touch—until she realized the warmth was caused by the heat of the day, rather than any life force within.

She let the hand she had been holding fall limp to the ground.

Brian was dead.

His body was lying in such a way that the right side of his face pressed against the ground. Dried blood stained the sand beneath, though not as much as one might expect from the deep ugly wounds on his forehead. Lena glanced upward. Somehow—improbable as it seemed—he must have lost his balance on the scaffolding, gone over the side, and banged his head as he plummeted down.

Lena was not one to panic or give way to hysterics. Far from it. Often, jokingly, she referred to herself as "a tough old bird." Why, then, were her hands shaking, her body trembling? Brian Siminski was dead; nothing she or anyone else could do would ever change that.

The only thing to be done now was to hurry back to the house and dial 9-1-1. Even so she stood undecided. She hated to leave his body lying like that, exposed—the memory of Pal's rotting carcass, and the telltale vultures, was still fresh in her mind—but there was no help for it; stubborn, antiquated fool that she was, she did not own a cell phone.

Before making her way around the screenhouse she gave the body one last parting glance, as if to convince herself that she was not dreaming, that this was not a ghastly nightmare from which she would soon, joyfully, awaken.

Wait. What was she thinking? How could she have forgotten? The other young man. Eric. Where in heaven's name was he?

Well, he wasn't here, obviously. Not outside. And not in the anteroom.

Come to think of it, had she seen him at all that day? She hadn't noticed the van's arrival that morning; she had been taking her shower around that time. She did see it leave the bog sometime before noon, and return an hour or two later, but hadn't paid much attention as to who was inside. Even if she hadn't seen Eric at that point, she would have assumed that he had for whatever reason remained behind at the screenhouse.

He certainly was nowhere in sight now. Chances were he hadn't shown up for work at all.

CHAPTER XV
A New Wrinkle

On the darkened portico all was still. It must be after midnight, Cheryl thought. She had lost all track of time, ever since Lena had burst through the door to make her frantic 9-1-1 call. Cheryl had listened, stunned, to Lena's frenzied recitation. And then the two of them had waited. The cruisers arrived first, then the ambulance. By the time they had come and gone dusk had fallen.

Somewhere deep within the swamp, in widely separated quarters hundreds of yards apart, a family of coyotes yodeled back and forth to one another, plaintively, their ululations an affirmation of kinship and mutual dependence. High above the bog the moon, like a spectral face drawn to the eerie melody, peered down from behind a thin veil of clouds—portent of the rain meteorologists had forecast for the wee hours.

Portentous, too, was the breeze that wafted across the bog in faint exhalations, the labored breathing of a heat-weary earth. The breeze, though it filliped the tips of the lilacs and rhododendrons massed around the portico, scarcely reached the spot where Cheryl stood alone, next to the coffin of light that spilled through the living room window. The moist air the breeze brought was heavy, scented with must, and did nothing to discourage the myriads of mosquitoes that pestered her.

As if prompted by the yowling of the coyotes, a bull frog, mired in the stagnant waters of a ditch in the bog behind the house, joined in, adding a sonorous bass to the roundelay: *Jug o' rum. Jug o' rum.*

The mosquitoes continued to annoy, as much by their shrill

whining as by their stinging bites. If only the frog would devote his energies to gulping down mosquitoes rather than attempting harmony with the coyotes! If he must open his mouth, let it be for a useful purpose.

She stood the insects as long as she could until conscious of the risk she was taking, of the death they now and then, particularly at this time of year, delivered—Eastern Equine Encephalitis, fatal to fifty percent of those infected, often leaving the surviving fifty percent permanently impaired (how many times had she preached all this to Lena?)—she turned and reentered the house. She found Lena in the library; it was the sanctuary her friend sought whenever she felt deeply troubled. Lena sat upright in her chair, her gaze as vacant as the fireplace it was directed at.

"Time for bed?" Cheryl ventured. She was concerned by the older woman's haggard aspect, so unlike her usual self.

Lena shook her head. Her eyes remained fixed on the cold hearth.

"You must be tired."

"I am," Lena replied.

"Afraid you won't sleep?"

"Afraid I will." She looked up at the younger woman. "I'm not up to facing my dreams."

"Lena, you're not to blame for what happened."

"Phyllis Baker seems to think I am."

"That's absurd. The woman's in shock; from what you've told me she was very close to her nephew. Your phone call, so unexpected… She's not responsible for what she says. Give her time and she'll realize how unfair it is to hold you accountable for the accident." She went over and patted her friend's shoulder. "It's only human nature to blame the messenger."

"I still don't see how it could have happened," Lena, for the hundredth time, said.

"Lena, stop torturing yourself. It could've been loss of balance brought on by vertigo. Or just carelessness. Maybe he disturbed a hornets nest and got distracted fighting them off. Maybe the sun got in his eyes. There are any number of ways he could have fallen off that scaffolding. Chances are we'll never know. You'll just have to accept that." To change the subject she asked: "Where's Marmalade?"

Lena rose from her chair. "Upstairs, most likely. He can't stand my fidgeting; it gives him angst. He bore it as long as he could, then fled the room in a pique. I can't say as I blame him." As if to prove her point she began, like a caged beast, to pace back and forth.

"Can I get you something?" Cheryl asked. "You hardly touched your supper. I could warm something up."

Lena shook her head.

"A glass of wine? It might help calm your nerves."

Lena smiled wanly. "No thank you, dear. Not tonight." She continued to stare at the fireplace, at the soot-blackened reredos, as if seeking to find meaning there, something beyond cold comfort.

The phone rang. Cheryl hurried into the kitchen to answer it.

Who could it be? Lena asked herself. The police? Hadn't they already asked every conceivable question, twice if not three times? Phyllis? She hoped not; she could not deal with the woman again that evening—or rather, by now, morning.

Cheryl's voice carried from the other room. "May I ask who's calling?"

So it was not the police, nor Phyllis. Who then?

"For you, Lena," Cheryl called out.

Reluctantly—what now?—Lena left the library for the kitchen.

"Mildred Russell," Cheryl said as she handed her the phone. "Eric's mother."

Lena accepted the instrument but held it at a distance from her ear, as if it were some newfangled gadget whose exact purpose she could not quite fathom. Finally, steeling herself for what she instinctively knew could only be bad news, she brought it close to her face. "Yes?"

"Mrs. Lombardi, forgive me for calling so late but I'm frantic about my son. I don't know what to do. He hasn't come home."

"I don't understand," Lena said. "What time did he leave?"

"Why, this morning. Brian picked him up the usual time, around twenty past six. I work two jobs; I didn't get home myself until half past nine this evening. I found the supper I always have ready for him still in the refrigerator. Lasagna and a salad with Italian dressing and apple pie for dessert."

"A date?" Lena ventured, tentatively, remembering the scars.

"Eric doesn't have a steady girl friend. The girls he meets can't seem to get beyond his face, to see the sweet person he is within. I thought maybe he went off somewhere with Brian—once in awhile Brian takes him to a movie. Brian has been good to my son that way. Eric doesn't drive—because of the bad accident he was in when he was a teenager."

Eric's mother paused, evidently to catch her breath. In the lull Lena listened as the first, intermittent, drops of the rain that had been promised for the early morning hours began to plash against the house. She was about to say something when Mrs. Russell resumed.

"Eric's a good boy. He always phones me if he expects to be late. I waited until after eleven but he never called. I got worried so I called Mrs. Baker. She told me the terrible news about Brian and now I'm worried sick. Where is my son? What can have happened to him?"

"I don't know what to tell you," Lena said. "If your son was here today I never saw him. I think you'd better phone the police, Mrs. Russell."

She talked a while longer, not able to offer the woman any comfort, nonetheless trying to calm her fears. When she got off the phone she returned to the library. The beat of the rain was louder now, more steady. Normally Lena found its rhythms soothing. This time, however, it was like a coarse, uneven drumming in her ears, an irritant.

Cheryl, who was seated, glanced up at her friend and said, lifting her brows: "I caught the gist of your conversation. This is a new wrinkle."

"I don't know what to make of it," Lena replied. She sank into her chair. "Eric's mother claims that Brian swung by the house and picked her son up for work. Did they come directly here? Or did Brian leave Eric off somewhere on the way? Did they both show up here as usual? In either case, what's happened to Eric? Where is he?"

"I wonder…" Cheryl mused. "The few times you met Eric…you said he acted a little strange?"

"Kinda," Lena said, dubious. "I mean…he did suffer brain damage in the accident that disfigured him. He seemed, not exactly simple, but…peculiar. Perhaps *childlike* is the best way to describe him. Naive, maybe. Innocent. Ingenuous." She glanced at the younger woman. "What are you driving at? You're not implying…?"

"I'm not implying anything; I'm just supposing," Cheryl replied. "Suppose Eric witnessed Brian falling from the scaffolding. Or suppose he came upon him afterwards, lying on the ground dead. In either instance he might've 'freaked out'—for lack of a better term. 'Lost it' if you will. He might have fled in a panic into the swamp."

"I guess it's possible," Lena conceded. "But I seriously doubt it. I think he would have sought help instead. According to his mother he doesn't drive. But he would have run straight here, I feel confident of that."

"Or suppose he somehow caused the accident," Cheryl said. "Inadvertently. Seeing what he'd done, he might have panicked. Or," she said, drawing the word out, "he might have, for whatever reason—an argument maybe—deliberately pushed Brian. That would account for his disappearance. He could be hiding somewhere. You said you didn't check inside the screenhouse. He might have hid himself in there."

"I just don't know what to think," Lena said. "His face is hideously scarred; maybe his psyche is, too. I feel sorry for his mother. And for him, if he's in trouble. He seems like a nice enough fellow, not at all like a pirate. I wish now that I hadn't made fun of him, even if it was only behind his back."

"He's bound to turn up sooner or later," Cheryl said. "My guess is sooner. Listen to that rain. Even if he's someplace dry, he must be getting hungry." She rose from her chair and went over to the older woman and patted her on the shoulder. "Lena, I think it's time we both turned in."

CHAPTER XVI

A Visit from the Police

The following day saw continued rain throughout the morning, plus, in the afternoon, a visit from the police.

Officer Bolduc phoned from the station beforehand. Lena felt somewhat abashed taking the call; the last time she'd had dealings with the local constabulary (other than yesterday's 9-1-1 call) she had, flippantly, referred to the young man as "Officer Cold Duck." Well, he had given her just cause; she had been miffed at his obtuseness, or rather the obtuseness of his superior, who had failed to take seriously the information which, gratuitously, she had presented to them, concerning a heinous crime which, in the end—without *their* assistance—she had helped to solve.

But that was all water under the bridge.

At precisely ten minutes past three two officers arrived at her door—neither of them, thankfully, Officer Bolduc.

One, in plain clothes, flashed his badge and identified himself as Detective Something-or-other; Lena never did quite catch his name. It began with an A and sounded vaguely Armenian. Why not just think of him as Detective Armenian? That was close enough. Detective Armenian was of middle-age and middle height and had a paunch. His hair, streaked with gray, was cut short; he had close-set eyes and a muscular torso which, despite the spare tire, gave the overall impression of an aging drill sergeant. His manner, however, was excessively polite, a trait that spoiled the otherwise dour image.

The second officer, in uniform, was an attractive woman in her late twenties, of indeterminate ethnicity. She was equal in height to her companion, five feet eight or nine. Her flesh tone was beige; she had straight black hair, worn short under her officer's cap, and large brown eyes which, like a very young child's, seemed to gaze out upon the world with a sense of perpetual wonder. Her manner, though courteous, was curt. Detective Armenian introduced her as Officer Mills.

Lena invited them into the kitchen to sit at the table, while at the sink she continued washing and peeling the garden vegetables she had gathered fresh that morning: baby carrots, scallions, cucumbers, a head of lettuce that had survived the heat, and an early tomato. Preparing supper gave her something to do; it distracted her from the tragedy of Brian's untimely death and the shock of its having occurred on her property. Cheryl, who had previously made plans with Anthony to head down to Provincetown for the day (he was taking a mini vacation from his job as a research scientist for Ocean Spray), had offered to remain with her instead, but Lena insisted that her friend stick to her original arrangement.

"There's no sense in two of us moping about," Lena said. "Marmalade will have enough on his hands—or should that be paws?—just coping with me. 'Moping' and 'coping'; I'm a poet but don't know it."

"But your feet show it; they're Longfellows," Cheryl quipped. It was a favorite joke between them, an old chestnut, which no doubt long ago should have been relegated to the junk heap of worn-out witticisms—but perhaps what Lena needed to see her through this time of stress and sadness were banalities, the tried and true.

"We have a few questions we'd like to ask you," Detective Armenian said. Despite the invitation to sit, he and Officer Mills remained standing. "Before we begin I have to inform you that Brian Siminski's death may not have been accidental. In fact, we're treating it as a homicide."

"Oh dear," Lena said. She placed the carrot she was about to peel on the cutting board and turned to face the officers. "I don't understand…"

"Because our investigation is on-going we can't reveal all the details," the detective said. (How would the police ever manage without all those formulaic phrases of theirs? *On-going investigations, persons of interests*.) "But we can tell you that according to the medical examiner, Mr. Siminski's head wounds are not consistent with a fall. He appears to have been bludgeoned to death."

"But I found him under the scaffolding," Lena protested, realizing, even as she spoke, the absurdity of what she was saying. What difference did it make, if he had been bludgeoned to death, where she found him?

She was too stunned to think clearly.

Seeing her distress, Detective Armenian suggested that she sit, and kindly drew a chair from the table. Lena sank onto it, then stiffened, attempting to absorb the import of the detective's words. Bludgeoned to death…

When she had sufficiently composed herself the detective continued, in that soothing manner of his which in the past, Lena reflected, must have lulled many a suspect, deceived many a culprit, into mistaking *soft-hearted* for *soft-headed*. "Mrs. Lombardi, please tell us what you know about Mr. Siminski. How long he'd been working for you, how you happened to hire him. Who, if anyone, was working with him. Who might have wished him harm."

"I can't think of anyone who might have wished Brian harm," Lena said. "I really know very little about him. He was just a young man I hired to do some repairs to my pump house. A friend of mine, his aunt, Phyllis Baker, recommended him. I took an instant liking to Brian; he's—he was—a hard worker, good at what he did, and he seemed honest. And so after he finished the pump house I asked him to fix up my screenhouse."

She gave him the dates, as far as she could remember, conscious that Officer Mills was dutifully jotting down on a pad of paper everything she said. Lena deliberately omitted mention of Eric Russell. She was curious to see how this Detective Armenian would broach the subject. By now Eric's mother would have notified the police that her son was missing (assuming he hadn't returned home). But would the left hand of the police know what the right hand was doing?

"There was someone else working with Mr. Siminski," the detective said. "Eric Russell." It was a statement, not a question. Though delivered in an offhand, almost avuncular manner, Lena sensed an undertone, an edginess, as if whatever she said in response might be vital to the investigation. "When did you last see him, Mrs. Lombardi?"

"The day before yesterday," Lena said, and explained that she could not say for certain, one way or the other, whether he had shown up for work yesterday. She related what little she knew about Brian's helper—which was next to nothing—concluding with the phone call she'd received from his mother.

If Brian's death was not accidental—if he had been murdered—then of course Eric Russell, whether amongst the missing or not, was the obvious suspect. The police could hardly think otherwise. Lena herself did not know what to think. Her mind was still reeling from the shock of finding Brian dead, and now from the knowledge that his death was not the tragic accident it had at first appeared to be.

Detective Armenian stepped to the window above the sink and peered outside. "It's stopped raining," he said. "We'd like you to show us where you found the body, and answer a few more questions, if you don't mind." As they were preparing to leave he added: "We'd also like to take a look inside the screenhouse."

Lena led the way in her pickup. The cruiser, Officer Mills at the wheel, followed close behind, scrupulously avoiding the puddles which Lena splashed through with puerile abandon. Surely the officers did not mind a little dirt on their cruiser; surely they would not be expected to wash down their own vehicle?

At the clearing Lena pulled up next to Brian's van, which, after all, was still there; no one, neither Brian's parents nor his aunt Phyllis, had had it removed—had, in their shock, possibly not given it a thought. Now, with the knowledge that Brian's death was the result of murder—or manslaughter; Lena found it hard to believe that anyone (Eric?) could have actually planned it—the police would want to go through the vehicle thoroughly. They might impound it, even, if they found anything remotely suspicious.

Officer Mills parked the cruiser off to one side, well away from the screenhouse. When Lena got out of the pickup Detective Armenian approached her, and in his soft-spoken way requested that she remain there until the evidence gatherers—who, on their way, should arrive any moment—had completed their work.

"They'll go over everything with a fine-toothed comb," he explained. "I want you to be present so that you can tell us exactly how everything was when you arrived here yesterday afternoon."

First to arrive were the EMTs who had carted off the body, their presence necessary, Lena assumed, to corroborate the testimony of the police officers who had likewise responded to Lena's 9-1-1 call. Those two individuals, in civilian clothing, arrived shortly after. The four, none of them officially on duty, formed a loose knot by the edge of the bog, patiently awaiting the technicians—whose job, never easy, had been made particularly difficult by last night's rainfall. The murderer—it must have been murder, if the medical examiner said so, though Lena still had difficulty accepting the fact—had received a lucky break from Mother Nature.

Unless of course it was poor Eric Russell who had, for whatever reason, killed his friend. If that were so, any evidence obliterated by the rain would not make much, if any, difference in the case.

It took the team of technicians roughly half an hour to scour the area around the spot where Brian's body had lain. Lena doubted whether they found anything of significance. Even without the rain the hard gravel surface would not have allowed for discernible footprints; last evening's activity—on the part of Lena, the EMTs, and the responding officers—would have erased faint impressions, had there been any. Then had come the heavy downpours. Even so, the killer (she had to get used to that word when thinking of the circumstances surrounding Brian's death!) might have grown careless and left something behind, some trace, some clue.

When the technicians had completed this, the initial phase of their investigation, Detective Armenian, after apologizing for keeping her waiting, asked Lena to show, by retracing her steps, exactly how she had discovered the body.

When she had done so he turned his attention to the screen-house. Out of habit Lena had, the previous evening after the ambulance and cruiser left, locked the door. Detective Armenian now asked her to unlock it.

As she was doing so the K-9 Unit arrived. The unit consisted of a cruiser, a police officer, and a dog on a leash. The dog, a muscular German shepherd, bounded from the vehicle, pranced about once or twice, then, tongue lolling, waited patiently for instructions from his human partner. They were not long in coming. The officer, after conferring briefly with Detective Armenian, reached into the vehicle and took out a plastic bag, from which he extracted a faded and well-worn baseball cap with the Red Sox logo emblazoned on it.

Lena could guess whose cap it was.

The police would have obtained the cap from Eric's mother—but only after the medical examiner's report. Had Mildred Russell, in handing it over, an inkling as to the true reason for their wanting the cap? Lena doubted if that were so. The poor woman must think the police were eager to find her son in order to return him safely home to her.

Did anyone in the general public besides herself know that Brian's death was deemed a homicide? Had his parents or aunt been told?

Lena would have been told out of necessity, so that the authorities could pursue their investigation at the crime scene. But the media may not have been informed, so as not to alert Eric, if he were hiding out. Perhaps the hope was that if Eric assumed that the police believed Brian's death was accidental he would eventually return home on his own.

The officer allowed the dog to sniff the cap. To what purpose, Lena could not fathom. Surely rain in such abundance as had fallen overnight would have obliterated any trace of Eric's spoor. Ah, but it had not rained inside the screenhouse—which is where, the dog leading the way, the police began their search.

They did not find Eric, living or dead, inside. They found something else, however—something important enough to warrant a bevy of technicians with kit bags to spend what to Lena seemed an inordinate length of time fossicking about. Though she was not privy to their findings, she learned—by, as she later explained to Cheryl, keeping her "eyes and ears open" (that is to say, by eavesdropping)—that blood stains had been located on the cement floor. The presumption was that the murder had occurred there, and the body moved outside, under the scaffolding, to make it appear as though Brian had fallen from a height.

Would a clever murderer expect to get away with such a ploy? Probably not. Anyone with even a rudimentary knowledge of forensics would know that the police would eventually—almost immediately—see through the stratagem. As indeed they had.

But was Eric clever?

Of course, a clever murderer may have resorted to the ruse merely to gain time. Had Lena discovered Brian's body inside the screenhouse, she would at once have recognized foul play, and the police would have begun their crime investigation then and there, well before the rain, while the evidence was still fresh. Lena had read somewhere—a hundred places probably—that the first twenty-four hours were vital to an investigation. Well, those twenty-four hours had long since elapsed.

CHAPTER XVII
Obsequies

Brian's funeral was held a week later in Wareham.

Lena, no fan of long-winded, sanctimonious sermons that left the listener bloated with pieties and platitudes, eschewed the church service but attended the graveside ceremony. The plot chosen for Brian's final resting place (as if the dead needed rest!) overlooked a quiet pond—the Mill Pond, Lena assumed it was called, since beyond it, across Route 28, she could see, plainly, the Mill Pond Diner. Brian, she had found out in the short time she knew him, appreciated nature, its creatures and its beauties. There were ducks and geese in the pond; it would be visited, throughout the seasons, by other wildlife as well—a fitting spot for one who loved the outdoors.

Despite the sweltering heat thirty or forty mourners were present. Lena derived solace in observing among them four of five tearful-eyed young ladies. Brian, she surmised, had been—despite his extreme shyness—popular with at least these members of the opposite sex. A confirmed *bon vivant* herself, she hoped that the young man, in his brief sojourn on planet earth, had sowed his share of wild oats.

After the ceremony Brian's parents—the father tall, heavy-set (he was after all Phyllis Baker's brother, there could be no doubt of that!) with a grizzled beard and a morose expression not, Lena guessed, entirely occasioned by his son's murder but rather a permanent fixture; the mother contrastingly small of frame, red-faced and blowzy (a condition brought on, presumably, as much by the consumption of alcoholic beverages as by grief at her son's untimely demise)—invited everyone to Vel's on Route 28 for sandwiches and dessert.

At the restaurant Phyllis Baker made a point of coming up to Lena and apologizing for having, in her grief, lashed out.

"Pshaw," Lena responded. "I've already forgotten it; you were understandably upset." Pouring herself a cup of steaming hot coffee, which she took black, and grabbing a chicken-salad sandwich from the buffet, she seated herself at a corner table. Phyllis sat across from her.

"Brian was like a son to me," Phyllis said. "I just can't believe that...something like this happened."

"Has there been any sign of the other young man—Eric Russell?"

Phyllis shook her head. She had brought with her only coffee to the table. She stirred it listlessly, without interest, as if the cup were empty, and it, the saucer, and the spoon were merely stage props, there for no other purpose than to lend verisimilitude to an already tedious scene.

"Do you have any idea what *did* happen?" Lena asked. "I knew your nephew for such a short time, but I had grown to like him. I know nothing of this Eric, what sort of person he might be. What he might be capable of." She took Phyllis's hand in her own and pressed it. "You understand that I'm not being just idly curious. Whatever did happen to Brian happened while he was on my property, doing work for me. The rational part of me knows, of course, that I am in no way to blame. But at the same time another part of me seeks absolution. If, as the police insist, Brian's death was not accidental, I have to know who, then, is responsible."

Phyllis nodded her head slowly, as if in empathy with the sentiments Lena was expressing. The action caused her chin to quiver, with the rocking motion of a rubber boat on pontoons with the incoming tide.

In a soft voice—so as not to be overheard?—she said by way of prelude: "Brian did not get along with his parents. Jim—my brother—and Carolyn weren't entirely to blame. Brian was...he could be...difficult."

"He did seem strange at times," Lena said. "I don't mean that in a negative way. But it seemed to me as if something was eating away at him. He reminded me of a person who for whatever reason is not at peace with himself."

"You know about the accident?" Phyllis said, her intonation half statement, half question.

"The one in which his brother was killed? Brad, I think his name was?"

Phyllis nodded, setting her chin in motion again. "Brian was never the same after that. Up until then he had been a normal teenager, interested in sports, not too interested in school." She broke off, as if reluctant to further characterize her nephew, whose body, after all, they had only minutes before laid in the ground.

"Tell me about the accident," Lena said. "There were other boys involved, weren't there?"

"Three others," Phyllis said, "besides Brian and Brad. Brian was only sixteen. He'd been so looking forward to getting his driver's license. But after the accident he wanted nothing to do with cars. It wasn't until about five years ago that out of necessity he learned how to drive and bought that old van. Brad was eighteen at the time of the accident. It was his car." She twirled the spoon around in her cup, and finally took a sip. "Eric Russell was one of the others. You've seen what the accident did to him."

"I got the impression that Brian took him under his wing, so to speak. He seemed protective of Eric," Lena said.

"He was. Very protective."

"And yet," Lena went on, "the police obviously think that Eric is somehow responsible for what happened to Brian. How do you square the two?"

"I don't," Phyllis confessed. "Unless..." She shrugged before continuing. "Unless Eric somehow snapped."

"He seemed docile enough, the few times I saw him," Lena said. "Could it be that he had mood swings?" She recalled his antic behavior, his prancing about at the prospect of spraying insecticide on the powder post beetles.

"Not that I know of," Phyllis replied.

Lena took a bite from her sandwich. Her companion was not eating, she noted. For Phyllis, as with so many overeaters, loss of appetite was evidently part of the mourning process. Lena felt a pang of compassion for the old sow.

"I understand that another boy besides Brad was killed in the accident."

"Jacob Britto," Phyllis said. "He was twenty." She sighed. "The other boy, Jay O'Sullivan, was the only one who wasn't a minor. He was twenty-one. They had all been drinking, of course. The accident took place a few miles up the road from here in Middleborough, near Sisson's Diner. The car went out of control around the bend. Jay—he was the only one who was not killed or badly hurt—told the police that Brad was the driver. It was Brad's car, and the police believed Jay. But Brian told me—this was years afterward—that Brad was too sick from the liquor to drive, and that it was actually Jay who was at the wheel. It was Jay, too, who bought the liquor in the first place."

"So he got off scot free," Lena said. "Physically and legally."

Phyllis nodded. Suddenly she frowned. "Come to think of it, I don't recall seeing Jay at the graveside service. Or at the funeral parlor. You'd think he'd have the decency to at least show up."

"Maybe he didn't hear about what happened," Lena said. "He may have moved away from the area."

Phyllis shook her head. "He's still around. He works at one of the big box stores. Lowe's, I believe." She lifted her shoulders in a half shrug. "Maybe he's afraid to face my brother and his wife. Jim never talks about the accident, but he's no fool. He must blame Jay to some extent. He was the oldest; he was the one most responsible. Jim has a temper. Come to think of it, it was wise of Jay not to show his face today."

CHAPTER XVIII
Stymied

At five foot seven Lena Lombardi was by no means a large women. Though slender of build, she was solid, having spent an active life on the cranberry bogs. For a woman in her mid seventies she possessed, under normal circumstances, a hearty appetite. She was an excellent toper, too; she could drink any man under the table. Well, any man of corresponding age, if the drink of choice was wine and the man not a hopeless drunkard. Of late, however, she hardly touched the stuff; as for food, Lena could no longer be counted among the trenchermen.

Cheryl Fernandes suspected that she knew the underlying cause of this sudden change.

"You're off your feed," she remarked, as they sat at the breakfast table the morning following Brian's funeral. "Lately you've eaten hardly anything; for the past ten minutes I've watched you pick at your eggs. I must say you've done an excellent job of mutilating the yolks." As if to demonstrate proper mastication, she took a heaping forkful from her own plate and shoved it into her mouth. When she finished swallowing she said: "Even Marmalade eats more than you."

At mention of the cat Lena's face broke into a fond smile. "That's not saying a great deal, dear. You know what an absolute glutton he is."

Ignoring the remark, Cheryl said: "I can't remember the last time we enjoyed a glass of wine together."

"I'm in fine fettle, dear, if you're concerned for my health. At any rate, physically. Spiritually there's room for improvement." She

106

shoved her plate away from her, nudging it toward the center of the table. "Consider: a brutal murder has been committed on my property. The victim is someone I knew. A young man whom I'd grown quite fond of. The fact that his murderer is on the loose irks me."

"Surely it's his friend Eric who's responsible for Brian's death," Cheryl said. "It's only a matter of time before the police apprehend the poor wretch."

"Don't be so sure of his guilt, dear. Eric doesn't strike me as the type who can fend for himself. Not for more than a day or two." She reached over and took a bite from the food on her plate and chewed it slowly, as if to placate her friend. "At first I might have agreed with you. But it's been more than a week now since he went missing. Through no fault of his own he doesn't drive; we can assume that wherever he is, he arrived there on foot. Unless he broke into a summer cottage somewhere close by and has been cowering there ever since, I fear the worse."

"What is your theory, then?"

"I have no theory." She toyed with the mound of cold food on her plate. "I'm stymied."

"Hence the loss of appetite?"

Lena nodded. "Foolish of me, I know." Abruptly she rose from the table. She scraped the remainder of her meal from the plate into the compost bucket that was stored, pending later disposal outside, in a cabinet under the sink.

"The raccoons will have a field day with that," Cheryl observed.

"If the coyotes don't find it first," Lena said. She turned and faced her friend. "I'm glad we had this conversation, dear. You've made me realize how truly foolish I've been." She approached the table to gather up the remaining dishware. Motioning Cheryl to remain seated she added: "I've made up my mind that the time for moping about is past. From this day forward I intend to be my old self again." She carried the dishes to the sink.

Cheryl left the table and went over to the counter, where she gently nudged her aside. "My turn."

"If you insist. But I'll dry," Lena said.

"You don't fool me, Lena. About returning to being your old self.

You've got something up your sleeve."

Lena shook her head. "This time you're wrong, dear. As I said, I'm stymied. But that doesn't mean I won't await developments." She received a dripping plate from Cheryl and dabbed it dry with a dish towel. "In the meantime I think I'll go and pick some blueberries. Care to join me?"

Buckets swinging at their sides, the two women set off down the dirt track that ran parallel to the bog. Had they wished, they could have ridden in the pickup as far as the screenhouse, but they chose to travel by shanks' mare instead. Despite the summer heat the day was inviting: low humidity, a light westerly breeze, blue sky festooned with high, billowy clouds that promised, and delivered now and then, pockets of refreshing shade. In short, a perfect day for walking outdoors. The extra exercise would do them good.

Cheryl had on a pair of old leather boots; frayed jeans; a faded green top with long sleeves as protection against poison ivy, thorns, ticks, and stinging insects; and a cap with an oversized visor; Lena a floppy straw hat and a man's blue cotton shirt (it had been her husband's long, long ago) tucked into tan slacks, patched with swatches of mismatching brown, which were themselves tucked into the tops of boots that, in Lena's own words, "had seen better days," but were just the thing for trudging through the muck of a New England swamp.

"We look like a pair of country hicks," Cheryl observed.

"We *are* a pair of country hicks," Lena said.

A tractor from the growers' service had recently mown the vegetation along the shore and on the dikes. Decapitated grass, noxious weeds, and wild flowers alike lay strewn in the ruts of the dirt track; sap leaking from the bruised vegetation perfumed the air with the sickly-sweet scent of incipient decay. Honey bees from wooden hives placed strategically on various clearings near the bog buzzed about angrily, as if resentful of such wanton destruction.

"Drat!" Lena exclaimed.

Cheryl gave her a sidelong glance. "Forget something?"

"My .22 pistol." Lena grimaced. "I had a feeling I was overlooking something when we left the house."

"Planning on shooting muskrats?"

"Don't be silly, dear. I was thinking of bigger game. With a murderer running around loose a pistol might come in handy."

"Is it Eric Russell you have in mind? You don't really think he's lurking in the swamp, do you? Subsisting on frogs' legs and wild berries."

"Now you're being a wisenheimer again," Lena complained. "I'd feel better if I was packing, that's all."

"Packing?"

"Heat. 'Packing heat.' It's an expression gangsters use, meaning 'carrying a gun.'"

"It's an expression gangsters used back in the 1920s," Cheryl said. "These days it comes across as rather dated."

"I think it's rather colorful," Lena protested. "Just because an expression is old doesn't mean it's hopelessly outdated. Think of Shakespeare. He's been dead four hundred years. That doesn't prevent people from quoting him."

"This morning at breakfast you promised you'd be your old self again, and you're certainly keeping your word," Cheryl said, laughing. But as they approached the screenhouse her demeanor grew more serious. "It's creepy, knowing a young man in the prime of life met violent death just a few feet from where we're standing."

"Let's not dwell upon it, dear. Not for the next few hours anyhow." Lena plunged headlong into the swamp, as if seeking sanctuary there from the horrors of the world.

CHAPTER XIX
Sweet Baby

He pulled up to the curb on a narrow side street away from the main drag—not too far away, though, not in this scumbag of a neighborhood—where he felt confident he would be neither recognized, nor mugged, and walked the rest of the way on foot.

Although born and bred on Cape Cod, and a lifelong resident there (sea and salt air suited him fine, not to mention the influx of summer babes), at the age of thirty-one Jay O'Sullivan was no stranger to New Bedford's south end. And although not what you might call an habitué, he was familiar with any number of dimlit corners, back alleys, cul-de-sacs, and dumpsters overflowing with refuse, couched in deepest shadow, beyond the purview, the prying eyes, of officialdom. Hadn't he scored drugs at such venues dozens of times? Potent stuff, and a lot cheaper than anything available on the Cape. The whores were cheap, too, though with them (as with the dope) you had to be careful; you might get more than you bargained for.

Today Jay's purpose for being in the south end was, as always, to make a purchase. On this occasion, however, it wasn't drugs or feminine affection he was looking to buy. The object of today's quest, though equally illicit, and as potentially deadly, was a commodity far more durable.

The address he had obtained (from doubtful sources) was three blocks away from where he had parked his car. It was in a scruffy area, no doubt about that, bad even by the standards of New Bedford's south end. That's why he had insisted on the deal taking place in broad daylight; as with the whores, you could never be too careful.

As he approached the row of tenement buildings his heart began to palpitate; he could taste the dryness in his mouth. *Calm yourself, old buddy. Everything's gonna go smooth.* He rubbed the sweat from his palms onto the fabric of the long, baggy pants he had slipped into that morning in lieu of shorts—you could conceal things in baggy pants which you could not easily hide in shorts—and patted the bulge in his pocket created by the wad of twenties he had been instructed to bring. The bills were still there, as of course he knew they would be. Even so he breathed a sigh of relief; he would not like to contemplate the consequences of showing up at the rendezvous even a buck short.

He readily found the number of the building he was seeking, but did not so readily venture inside. One glance at the antiquated pile was enough to tell him it was a potential death trap: a six-family tenement so dilapidated that one or two taps with a wrecking ball would be sufficient to send it tumbling to the ground. Or never mind a wrecking ball. The next nor'easter, or even a potent fart, would do the trick.

With dismay he eyed the sagging roof, the peeling paint, the curtainless windows. Several of the windows, lacking screens, had cracked or missing panes, inviting insects to enter and toddlers to tumble out. From a window of an apartment on the top floor a corroded air conditioner jutted out at a rakish tilt, its rectangular butt mooning the street below.

Before mounting the stoop he took a moment to step back from the curb onto the pavement and, craning his neck, peered upward, gawking like a country hick. Did he really want to go through with this?

Across the street an ancient crone, mumbling to herself, came hobbling along the sidewalk, weaving from side to side like a huge misshapen beetle—in this shit hole of a neighborhood, no doubt a dung beetle. Jay snickered at his little witticism. Stalling for time—he was in no hurry to enter the portals of hell—he scrutinized her more closely. In spite of the heat she was clothed from tip to toe entirely in black, from the woven scarf covering her hair and knotted under her withered chin, to the cracked leather shoes in which she scuffed along the pavement: as if she were in perpetual mourning. In mourning for what, though? A long deceased spouse? A son lost at sea—or more likely, to an overdose in some sordid back alley? The crucified Christ? Her lost youth? All of the above?

Devoid of teeth, her wrinkled mouth, in constant motion, was soft and flabby like a cow's ass.

Jay had seen a cow's ass on a farm once when he was a kid, had watched in fascination as, chewing contentedly at one end, the animal simultaneously shit from the other. When the old woman spotted Jay standing there apparently without purpose, and looking at her, she came to a full stop, and stared.

Jay stared back.

Who does she think she is? He wondered. The resident banshee? Why did she stand there gaping at him? She was giving him the shivers, the old battle-ax—like she was measuring him for a coffin. Finally, freaked out by the implacable vacancy of her eyes, he tore his gaze from hers and, heedless of the unknown hazards that might lie before him, bounded up the wooden stoop. The sagging wooden steps groaned under his weight but held.

The door at the top of the steps was not locked, was in fact ajar. Before entering the building he glanced over his shoulder at the crone. She stood there still, on the sidewalk, regarding him as if he were a specimen she was about to pin to a collection board, her lips all the while in rapid motion. Mouthing curses? Or about to let slide a cascade of manure? The old hag! Giving *him* the evil eye. He felt like throwing her the finger in return. But in this neighborhood that might not be a good idea. She might, after all, be somebody's grandmother. Somebody who might not appreciate the gesture.

Dismissing her from his mind (no easy task; she gave him the heebie-jeebies), he pushed through the door and stepped inside.

The entryway, though dark and redolent of a medley of noxious odors, was not, contrary to his expectations, strewn with desiccated corpses, although the two wraithlike figures sprawled in the shadows next to the stairwell, whom he nearly trod upon, might have passed as such, or at least as the mummified remains of the long-forgotten dead. As his eyes adjusted to the diminished light he saw that the two were indeed alive, if just barely: mere children—a boy about eight and a girl perhaps a bit older.

Pale, scrawny waifs. In need of a good meal and a good scrubbing, not to mention fresh air and the healthful rays of the sun. And, judging by the sorry state of their outfits, a visit to the nearest Salvation Army or Goodwill store might also be in order.

Had he ever laid eyes on such skinny ragamuffins? Perhaps; a dim recollection of photos he had seen of the Great Depression wavered in his consciousness. Were they deformed, diseased, or merely starved? He gave a mental shrug. The two were no concern of his. Like creatures disturbed from beneath a rotting log, they stared at him with listless eyes as he squeezed past; by the time he began to climb the stairs they had already lost interest and resumed the play he had interrupted: torturing a maimed cockroach held captive in a cardboard box.

The cockroach reminded Jay of the old dung beetle on the street outside; there was a distinct family resemblance. Was she still standing out there on the sidewalk mumbling to herself, putting a hex on him?

The stairwell, its sole source of illumination a flyspecked skylight, reeked of stale cigarette smoke, urine, and rotting garbage. And something else. Marijuana, sure. But beyond that? Discarded fast-food containers constituted hazards to navigation on the stairs and on the second floor landing—which, luckily, was as high up as he needed to go. If he'd ever read Dante (he hadn't), he would have recognized this as one of the circles of Hell. Any farther up and he might have turned back.

As instructed beforehand, he rapped his knuckles three times against the door that stood to the left of the landing.

"It ain't locked," a woman's voice rasped from within.

Jay grasped the knob. It was disgustingly sticky. Whatever substance coated it stuck to his hand like the viscous paste he used to sneak into his mouth in first grade whenever his teacher wasn't looking; the memory, coupled with the stench in the landing, made his gorge rise.

He pushed the door inward. A young woman—she might have been seventeen or eighteen—sat lounging on a tattered sofa facing the doorway. She appeared to be the only person in the room. Jay shoved the door behind him and stood by the threshold while he took in his surroundings.

Other than the sofa and a scarred wooden chair or two the room was bare of furniture. But not of filth. A threadbare carpet, cratered with cigarette burns, the greater portion of its surface stained like an abstract painting executed by a demented artist, covered two thirds of the floor's surface. The rest, around the edges, was linoleum. Where it wasn't stained the carpet was a dull green; the linoleum might once have been yellow.

The prevailing odor here was a mixture of tobacco, marijuana, and something else, something less definable. A buildup of garbage perhaps. Or a dead body behind the sofa. Or maybe it was just that the toilet in the bathroom needed cleaning. In the wall to the left of the sofa stood two doors, both of them shut. If one of the doors led into the bathroom, with any luck it would remain shut.

Funny how the mind works: the room, the stench, the shabbiness, reminded Jay of a figure from his childhood, someone he hadn't thought of in years: Mr. Melloni. Old Mr. Melloni was a grubby, ill-shaven widower who lived alone in a tumble-down house at the end of the street. A decorated veteran of World War II, Mr. Melloni was a little crazy. He, too, lived in filth, though nothing like this. Mr. Melloni knew that his house was dirty and liked to joke about it. He'd stand among the weeds in his junk-filled yard and sing a little ditty:

> *I shit in Spain*
> *I shit in France*
> *Before I shit in here*
> *I'll shit my pants.*

Bad enough just breathing the air in here, Jay thought, never mind taking a dump. He took a step forward, then halted. It might be a good idea to remain close by the door.

Without fluttering a lash the woman eyed him steadfastly, in the speculative way a cat stares at a mouse. Jay, in return, eyed her. This was not the reception he had expected.

Her skimpy outfit, diaphanous and none too clean, made a feeble pretense of covering her nakedness. The languid arms flung across the top of the sofa were intended, he guessed, to imply moral lassitude; they seemed instead a crude mockery of Jesus on the cross. Her legs, sprawled at an angle like the top of an old-fashioned milk carton being slowly pried apart, conveyed their own sordid message.

Jay—no rocket scientist, but no babe in the woods either—recognized a set up when he saw one. *One false move, buddy, and you're in big trouble.* A wrong word, an unwise gesture, would give our fair lady's pimp a pretext to burst into the room and shake him down.

Maybe he'd already made his false move: coming here in the first place.

He licked his lips nervously.

"I'm here to see Rodrigue," he said, keeping his voice, despite the dryness, steady.

"Rodrigue ain't here." The words scraped against her throat like sandpaper along a rusty blade. Too many cigarettes? Or had she damaged her vocal cords screaming?

"I have an appointment," Jay said. "Rodrigue is supposed to be here."

"Well, he ain't."

"Yeah, I can see." He turned to leave. "I'll come back some other time."

"What's yuh hurry?" She brought an arm down from the top of the sofa and patted the cushion next to her. Her fingernails were painted green. Or was that fungal scum? "Rodrigue'll be along sometime," she said. "You can wait for him here."

"Some other day maybe," Jay said. "Right now I got errands to run."

She stuck out her lips: a saucy attempt at a pout, perhaps, though the effect was more like a primate in heat. "Stay an' keep me company," she insisted. "We can have a little something together. A drink maybe."

"Like I said, I gotta go."

He opened the door to the landing; before he had a chance to step out of the room he heard, behind him, an inner door pop open.

He spun around on his heels.

A tall, thin man stood facing him, a gun in his hands.

"This what you come for?" the man asked.

Jay nodded.

"Let's see your money," Rodrigue said.

When, ten minutes later, Jay left the apartment, he had a new, larger bulge in his pocket to replace the wad of twenties. This bulge had a name, one he'd picked on the spur of the moment as he scurried down the stairs: Sweet Baby.

She was, after all, his bundle of joy.

The two skeletons disguised as children were no longer at the bottom of the stairwell. He might not have given them a second thought—why should he? the two were nothing to him—were it not for the cardboard box with its crucified cockroach lying at the foot of the stairs. He nearly tripped over the box in his haste to exit the building.

The old crone was missing from the street, too. Maybe she had whisked the children away. To fatten them up. Like the witch in "Hansel and Gretel." They'd take some fattening.

When he got to his car he removed Sweet Baby from his pants pocket and placed her, along with the box of cartridges, in the glove compartment. His hand still felt sticky from the door knob. As soon as he got home he would give himself, and Sweet Baby, a bath. A good cleaning, to remove the stench of Rodrigue and his squalid digs, and the memory of the girl with the raspy voice.

CHAPTER XX
The Kettle Hole

At about the same time that Jay O'Sullivan was tooling east on Route 195 transporting Sweet Baby to her new home on the shores of Buzzard's Bay, Lena Lombardi and Cheryl Fernandes were deep in the swamp gathering blueberries.

"That's it," Cheryl announced, from behind a tall bush whose branches she had nearly denuded of fruit. "I don't have room for any more." She emerged into view, a bucket brimful to overflowing swinging from each hand.

Lena cast an amused glance at her friend's purpled lips. "Are you referring to the buckets or to your tummy, dear?"

"Both," Cheryl replied. She searched out a spot of level ground between tussocks before setting the buckets down.

"A bumper crop, that's for certain," Lena said. Having already reached her quota, she'd spent the intervening ten minutes plucking the plumpest berries one by one and popping them into her mouth. "I, too, have eaten my share. Now for the hard part: lugging these buckets to the house. I almost wish we'd driven to the screenhouse after all."

"We both agreed that we wanted the exercise," Cheryl reminded her.

"By the time we reach home we'll have had exercise aplenty. Maybe too much."

"Once we're clear of the swamp it won't be so bad," Cheryl reassured her. "Pushing our way through briars and brambles—not to mention poison ivy—and hopping from tussock to tussock, while at

117

the same time trying to balance a full bucket from each hand so as not to spill what we've picked: that's the part I don't especially care for."

"We could take a shortcut, dear. That is, if you don't mind getting your feet wet."

"They're already wet," Cheryl observed. "Look. My boots are caked with muck."

"The trail I have in mind skirts the fringes of a kettle hole. There are one or two places where we might find ourselves ankle deep. At least you'd be rinsing the muck off."

Recalling a harrowing escapade from the past in which she'd been led will-o'-the-wisp fashion by Lena through the swamp, Cheryl asked: "Any danger that we'll sink out of sight?"

"Goodness no! The bottom's solid—glacial deposit, you know. Hardpan. We'll be fine as long as we keep to the edge. The pond—the kettle hole itself—is fairly deep."

"Formed by the last glacier, correct?"

"Correct."

"A deep drop, if we stray from the edge?"

"Fairly deep. The trick is not to stray. Of course, if you prefer we can always go home the long way."

Cheryl shook her head. "I'm game; after all, you haven't gotten me killed yet—though there have been some pretty close calls."

"Pshaw," Lena declared. "Think of all the fun we've had. Why, that time—"

"Please don't remind me," Cheryl interrupted, with a grin, "or I might change my mind about the shortcut." Seizing hold of her two buckets she declared: "Lead on, Macduff."

"This trail seems fairly well worn," Cheryl observed as they neared the kettle hole. "Hunters, do you suppose?"

"More likely the hunted," Lena replied. "Deer and other animals use it to get to the kettle hole for water. Not many humans come this way. Not since the Indians. Or at least not since the early English settlers."

"Someone's been here," Cheryl said. "Look." She pointed to the ground a short distance ahead.

A brown paper bag, or what was left of it, lay caught in vegetation to one side of the trail, a few feet from where the water from the kettle hole overlapped the edge.

"Now how did that get here?" Lena wondered.

"Fishermen?" Cheryl ventured. "Though there's hardly room enough for someone to stand, never mind cast a line."

Leaving her buckets on dry ground Lena stepped up to the rumpled paper and peered down. "There's writing on it." Bending, she scooped it up. As she did so something fell through the torn fabric. "Yuk."

"What is it?" Cheryl asked.

"A rotten apple."

Cheryl laughed. "Is that all? I thought it might be something truly gross. A rotten fish, for instance."

"Well, if you'll pardon the pun, there *is* something fishy here," Lena said. "Take a look at this." She handed the fragment over to Cheryl.

Cheryl set her buckets in the vegetation at her feet before—with a pronounced grimace—accepting the distasteful object. Turning it over a few times, she gave Lena a puzzled glance.

"Examine the writing," Lena instructed.

"…ric Russ…" she read. "Eric Russell!"

"His lunch bag. He must have come this way."

"You think so?"

"It certainly looks like it," Lena said.

"I don't know—an animal could have brought it here," Cheryl observed.

"It's *possible*," Lena said, though the way she drew out the word implied lack of conviction.

"If Eric left his lunch bag somewhere near the screenhouse—with the contents, or at least the apple, uneaten—after…whatever happened, an animal, a raccoon or fox or coyote or whatever might have grabbed it and dragged it into the swamp," Cheryl persisted. "That would explain the apple. An animal would eat a sandwich or piece of cake—whatever—but not the apple."

"Foxes eat apples," Lena said. "So do raccoons." She took the bag from Cheryl and examined it closely. "I'm no expert, dear, but I don't see any signs of an animal having torn this apart. No marks of tooth or claw. It looks like it fell apart from being exposed to all the rain we've had since Eric disappeared."

"Well, either Eric—or some other person—or an animal, or a bird—a crow possibly?—brought it here," Cheryl said. "We should hand it over to the police. Though I don't see what they'll be able to make of it."

Lena said nothing. She faced the kettle hole; planting her feet at the water's edge she gazed out across its quiet surface. She allowed her mind to drift far back into time; she imagined the pond being formed thousands of years ago—a colossal chunk of ice, acres in extent, dropped here by the glacier, over the course of millennia being buried in sand and gravel, then the glacier's slow retreat, and the chunk, still buried, melting, the gravel surface caving in, leaving a kettle-shaped hole to fill with ground water and become what it now was, a placid pond.

Remote, far from human habitation.

Since its formation by the glacier how many of her own species, how many human beings, had stood where she now stood—or anywhere on the pond's margin? Not many, she imagined. For the Algonquins it would have been just one of many such ponds, a place near which to hunt perhaps, though there were better places for that, more open, of easier access. The English settlers, the Pilgrims and their descendants, would have had little use for the pond. There were better places to farm, to graze livestock. There was no river or stream to power a mill; the pond was too deep to mine bog iron, too small, and isolated, for anything else.

And yet someone had stood here recently. Of that she felt certain, though she could not explain, even to herself, exactly why she felt that way. The presence of the paper bag of course. But something beyond that...

The very placidity...

In the bright sunlight the water sparkled as if sprinkled with di-

120

amond chips. The cramped strip of shoreline that like a bathtub ring lined the pond's circumference was plush with grasses, sedges, reeds, and tiny wildflowers, some of them rare, found only in Plymouth County and nowhere else in the world. Dragonflies, of many hues and sizes, flitted from stem to stem. These, too, the insects, and the shiny leaves of the plants, glinted in the sunlight.

A westerly breeze which elsewhere in the swamp hardly made its presence felt through walls of dense vegetation, here crinkled the pond's surface with gentle cat's-paws; the shadow of a passing cloud creeping from shore to shore darkened it. The cloud's passing was brief. As it moved onward, to other realms, sunlight showered onto the pond once again to paint the water blue and stipple its crimped surface with bits of shattered gems.

Had the cloud been an omen, Lena wondered—a hint of something dark, of what might lie hidden beneath the pond's surface? Or was she, in her dispirited mood, guilty of what Cheryl, the English professor, would term "the pathetic fallacy"—the attribution of human feelings to inanimate things?

She looked down at her hand, at the shard of brown paper bag she held between her fingers. Was this a significant clue, a piece of the puzzle? Or was it no more than what it was, a scrap of paper blown higgledy-piggledy by the wind? Not literally blown—the apple would have weighted the bag down. But blown figuratively, dragged hither and thither through briar and brush by an animal, or snatched from its original location and dropped here, by crow or gull. A meaningless occurrence. Like a dead leaf that by chance fell here instead of there.

She glanced at her friend.

Cheryl nodded toward the bag. "Shouldn't we be getting that to the police?"

"You caught me woolgathering," Lena apologized. "Do you think we ought to leave the bag exactly as we found it? In case it turns out to be important."

"I don't see how that would do any good," Cheryl said. "We've already compromised it as evidence, by moving it in the first place, and then by handling it."

"Oh dear. In trouble with the police again," Lena sighed.

Cheryl was not deceived. "You know perfectly well we can't be blamed for picking up a scrap of torn paper from the ground. How were we to know it was Eric's lunch bag?"

"What do you suggest we do?"

"I suggest that we get these berries home. Take a shower and change into clean clothes. Then drive to the police station."

"I like the part about the shower and clean clothes best," Lena said.

She carefully tucked the paper into her shirt pocket, then seized the wire handles of her buckets and leading the way continued the arduous trek through the swamp toward higher ground.

CHAPTER XXI
What the Policeman Said

"How much farther do we have to go?" The tone of voice was querulous, the person speaking the words obviously out of breath.

"Another hundred yards or so," Lena replied.

"You said that five minutes ago!"

"Yes, but I only said it then so that you wouldn't feel discouraged. This time I really mean it." She paused. "Well, perhaps two hundred yards."

"What in God's name were you doing all the way out here?"

"I told you. Picking blueberries. This is the shortcut."

"Shortcut!" A stream of expletives followed.

Poor Detective Armenian! His language was most unseemly, doubly so coming as it was from the lips of a law-enforcement officer. That time he called at her house with Officer Mills, the day after Lena reported finding Brian's body, he had seemed so mild-mannered, so soft-spoken. Well, judging by that spare tire of his—surely not a beer belly?—he was not the outdoorsy type, not accustomed, not of late anyhow, to strenuous exercise. This hike, besides taking its toll on him physically, was also adversely affecting his temper.

Lena smiled to herself. She should be the one complaining, not a robust policeman half her age. This was, after all, her second foray into the swamp that day. And it was she who was doing the bulk of the work, blazing the trail; all Detective Armenian had to do was follow. Which he did, charging head on, like a bull chasing a gazelle over open plains. She could hear him close behind, blundering through the brush, tearing his clothes, and most likely his flesh, on

123

briars and sharp branches, all the while muttering about this being a "wild goose chase."

Well, could she blame the poor fellow? Not adequately dressed for the task at hand, he was in danger of ruining, if not his entire outfit, then at least his shoes. And she had to give him credit for having agreed, however ungraciously, to see for himself the exact spot where she and Cheryl had found Eric Russell's lunch bag, or what was left of it.

And yet, if this expedition should cause irreparable harm to his clothing he had only himself to blame. In all fairness she had admonished him about the terrain, the absence of a real trail, the difficulty of getting there. The detective (she really ought to learn his name, she couldn't very well address him as "Detective Armenian," he might take offense; at this stage however she was too embarrassed to ask) had summarily dismissed her warning.

"I think I can manage," he said with a supercilious (dare one say chauvinistic?) grin and a cavalier wave of his hand.

The curl of his lip when he spoke the words irritated her. A by-product of male chauvinism, of course. Such hubris! Not hubris on the same level as Napoleon invading Russia, perhaps, or Custer at Little Bighorn, but hubris nonetheless. His thoughts probably ran along these lines: *Come now. If this little old lady in her seventies was able to make it to wherever it is and back, I guess I, a male in the prime of life, can, too. Piece o' cake. A complete waste of time, of course. But it wouldn't look good if I failed to follow up on every lead, however unlikely. It's best that I humor her. Leave no stone unturned, that sort of thing.*

"Here at last," she proclaimed as they came to the water's edge.

The detective, coming to a grateful halt and standing next to her, took a moment to catch his breath before casting his gaze at the kettle hole.

"This is the place?" he asked, incredulous. *This piss hole?* she imagined him thinking.

"Well, not the precise spot," Lena replied, somewhat indignant. What had the man expected? Lake Champlain?

She led him along the pond's margin to where, if memory served, she and Cheryl had come upon the lunch bag. Damn! She should have marked the spot with a hanky tied to a twig, or something to that effect, but hadn't thought to do so at the time. Too late now.

Ah! the apple.

"Right here," she said. "See, there's Eric's uneaten apple. It was in the bag when we found it. When I picked the bag up the paper fell apart and the apple dropped out and rolled onto the ground."

Detective Armenian, through pursed lips, slowly released the air from his lungs.

Not a happy camper, Lena thought. He thinks I've wasted his time. Perhaps I have.

At that point the detective surprised her by taking an evidence bag from his pocket. Stooping, he carefully nudged the piece of wizened fruit into it.

A snack for later? Lena was tempted to quip, but thought better of it. This was hardly an occasion for levity. No doubt he would show the apple to Eric's mother and ask her to identify it. It looked like a Granny Smith. The variety of apple might prove to be an important clue. If, for example, Eric had brought a Red Delicious to work with him on the day he disappeared, rather than a green Granny Smith. Or it could be that he would send the apple off to the lab for DNA testing.

Or, Detective Armenian might just be going through the motions of collecting evidence. In the parlance of the uncouth, he might be just "covering his butt."

"Can you recall whether either you or Ms. Fernandes touched the apple at any time?" he asked as he restored himself to an upright position.

"No," Lena replied. "I mean, I can say for certain that neither of us touched it. Like I said, the apple fell on its own accord and we just left it there. Do you think it's important?" she added eagerly.

He shrugged. His face was raddled, his clothes soaked with perspiration. "You want my honest opinion, Mrs. Lombardi? I personally don't think it's important. But until this case is solved, what I think or don't think is irrelevant. You found the bag and the apple, and I have to preserve them as best I can."

He mopped his brow with a white handkerchief. "I also have to mark this spot for possible future reference." Taking a short strip of yellow police tape, he looped one end around the trunk of a conveniently located shrub, and tied the other to a low-hanging branch.

"There," he said with obvious satisfaction.

Lena noticed too late, and didn't have the heart to inform him, that the shrub he had been handling was poison sumac.

"Do you have any theories?" she asked.

Detective Armenian looked at her with a blank expression. "Theories?"

"About the presence of the bag. How it got here. What it signifies."

"I've already expressed myself on that matter," came his curt reply. "If you'll kindly lead the way back to civilization…"

"Well, I have a theory," she declared. "A feeling, really. But a strong one."

"And what may your theory be?" the detective asked—not evincing any real interest in what her answer might be. He was just being polite, she realized. Irritatingly so.

To him she was just a foolish old lady. She would, nevertheless, be heard. "I think he's in there," she said, nodding toward the kettle hole.

With an expression of incredulity he directed his gaze first at the pond, then at her, as if to say, *are you nuts?*

"Eric Russell? In there?"

"That's my gut feeling," Lena said.

Detective Armenian shook his head. The message conveyed by the gesture was all too clear: *Nonsense! Of all the stupid notions…*

He brought out the handkerchief again and dabbed at the lacerations on his face and hands. Then, having taken a moment to ponder her words, he looked at Lena with renewed interest. "And how do you come to that conclusion?"

Oops. Was that a note of nascent misgiving she detected? Surely he didn't suspect *her* of foul play?

"It's not a conclusion," Lena corrected him. "Call it…intuitive."

"Intuitive." He repeated the word as if she had said *aliens from outer space told me* or *the knowledge came to me in a dream.* He looked

126

at her through narrowed eyes.

"Not just intuition," she insisted. "There's the fact of the lunch bag. What was it doing here, so close to the water's edge? And how did it get this far from the screenhouse?"

"I suppose there are any number of plausible explanations as to how it might have got here," the detective said. "We don't even know for certain that the lunch bag in question was the one that young Russell took to work with him on the day he disappeared. It might be his lunch bag from some other day." He paused. "In any case, I can't see any reason to speculate that he somehow ended up in the pond."

Besides, I have only your word that you came upon the bag in this location, he might have added. She could imagine what other thoughts must be coursing through his mind. *What an odd coincidence, that the very same person who claims to have discovered the murder victim (a man in her employ, found dead on her property) just happens to come upon what she purports to be his missing friend's lunch bag. And of all places, here…if you'll pardon my French…in the asshole of the world. She could very easily have planted the bag—along with the apple—so that she could later "discover" it in the presence of her friend. That is to say, if her friend isn't in cahoots with her to begin with. Oh, and she has a theory—that the missing Mr. Russell's body lies in the murky depths of yonder pond. Just a theory, mind you—with no logical explanation to back it up.*

Should she mention the passing cloud, the sensation of dread that had come over her as its shadow crept across the pond? No, of course not. What good would that do? It would take more than a mere hunch, a presentiment on her part, to penetrate the skepticism of this hard-nosed policeman. Still, she had to give it a try.

"Do you think Eric Russell is still alive?" she asked.

"I have no reason to believe otherwise," he replied, with little attempt to conceal his mounting impatience.

"You never met the young man," Lena said. "I did. He suffered a severe brain injury a number of years ago that left him impaired. Not retarded but…childlike. I don't believe he's capable of hiding out on his own. Someone may be helping him, of course. But who? The murderer? No, I think Eric's dead. Possibly in there." She pointed toward the kettle hole.

On the far side of the pond a half dozen turtles, lined up neatly in a row, were sunning themselves on the partially submerged trunk of a tree that had sometime in the past fallen victim to a violent storm. Painted turtles, in all probability. Though they could, just possibly, be the rare red-bellied terrapin, found, in New England, only in Plymouth County, and then only in a handful of locations.

Red-bellied terrapins.

Eric Russell.

Anything was possible.

When she turned from contemplating the turtles she found herself the object of Detective Armenian's own speculative stare.

"Mrs. Lombardi, supposing that your theory is correct, and Russell is in there." He gestured toward the pond. "How—according to your theory—did his body get there? Are you suggesting suicide?"

She shook her head. "I'm not suggesting anything, other than the feeling I have—it's only a feeling, but a strong one—that his body's at the bottom of the kettle hole. If I do have a suggestion to make, it's that you have a team of divers search for it."

"I can't do that, Mrs. Lombardi—not unless you provide me with more convincing evidence than just a gut feeling on your part." He paused to look at her expectantly.

The fool! Was he waiting for her to blurt out a confession?

She stepped away from the shoreline. "It's getting late. If we hope to make our way out of this swamp before dark it's time we got started."

"I'm sure you've had an exhausting day," Detective Armenian said as they began their outward trek. "One thing, though. Could you come to the station to make an official statement. About finding the lunch bag. And anything else you wish to tell us about your theory. Of course, it doesn't have to be until tomorrow."

"I'll be happy to give you a statement tomorrow," Lena said. *Along with a piece of my mind*, she was tempted to add, but didn't.

CHAPTER XXII
Habeas Corpus

"Marmalade grows lazier every day," Lena declared that evening when, after supper, she and Cheryl sat in the gazebo sipping lemonade.

The septuagenarian had, for the time being, sworn off wine—that is to say she had resolved not to take another sip until this case was solved one way or the other. For one thing, since the shock of finding Brian dead she hadn't been in the mood to partake of the grape. For another, she wanted to keep a clear head. She might not be the one to solve this mystery, but she at least wanted a shot at it. She owed that much to Brian. And, too, there was a touch of shamanism to her teetotalism, a pagan element: abstinence from wine was, if not equivalent to human sacrifice or even a burnt offering, her way of tossing a sop to the gods, an attempt at placation.

I'll give up something that is very dear to my heart, booze, if in return you'll provide me with a clue or two.

Of course, once this business was resolved—and it would be, even if she had to devote every waking hour for the remainder of her life to it—she would uncork a jeroboam of bubbly and get rip-roaring drunk.

"It's the heat," Cheryl said, referring to Marmalade's reluctance to move from one place to another.

"That, and the fact that he's gained weight," Lena observed sternly.

"I've been cutting down on his portions," Cheryl protested.

"But not on the number of portions," Lena said. "The frequency of feedings," she added, as if further clarification were necessary. Smiling, she reached over and patted her friend's hand. "Don't mind my petulance, dear. I'm positively pooped. And peeved as well."

"At Detective What's-his-name?" Cheryl commiserated. "For not taking your hunch seriously?"

"Not so much that," Lena said. "After all, I have no real evidence that Eric's body lies submerged at the bottom of the kettle hole, just a strong 'hunch,' as you so aptly put it. The police can't be expected to devote hours of their precious time, and hundreds or even thousands of tax payers' dollars, following up on what they no doubt perceive as the half-baked notion of a senile old lady." She paused. "I'm peeved because the damn fool suspects me of having killed Brian. Me, of all people!"

Taken aback by that last remark, Cheryl—privy to more than one dark secret from Lena's checkered past—had to bite her tongue. With an effort she puckered her face into what she hoped her friend would perceive as a sympathetic smile rather than an expression of amusement and said: "How absurd! Whatever makes him think the finger of guilt points at you?"

"Well, he hasn't come out and actually said so," Lena replied. "But I could tell from the tone of his voice—the way he narrowed his eyes when he looked at me—that I'm somewhere near the top of his list."

Forgetting that it contained not vintage wine but freshly-made lemonade instead, she lifted her glass to her lips and took a sip. The wash of sickly liquid against her tongue caused her to look at the glass askance, as if, victim of a cruel joke, she had been handed some-one's urine sample.

"But why?" Cheryl persisted.

Lena set the glass down and shrugged. "Suspicious circumstances, I suppose. Suspicious, that is, from the detective's perspective. Consider the facts: The murder occurs in *my* screenhouse. *I* report finding the body—as an accident, not a homicide. Days later, *I* just happen to be passing by the kettle hole, in a remote area of the swamp, where *I* just happen to come upon the missing Eric Russell's lunch bag. Oh, and here's the clincher: *I* express a hunch—with absolutely no evidence to back it up, other than a scrap of paper and a rotting piece of fruit—that Eric's body lies in that same kettle hole. And *I* urge him to send divers in search of it." She looked her friend squarely in the eyes. "How can he not suspect me? When you think of it in those terms, he would not be worthy of his badge if he didn't suspect me."

Cheryl pooh-poohed the notion. "If Detective What's-his-name did briefly consider you a suspect this afternoon—a circumstance I find hard to believe—he's bound to have seen the absurdity of it by now."

"I hope you're right, dear." She reached down and gently scratched behind Marmalade's ear. "I'll know better tomorrow, when I make my statement to the police."

As it turned out, Lena's prognostication of fuller knowledge on the morrow proved erroneous; the following day saw her no wiser vis-à-vis Detective Armenian and any suspicions, toward her or others, which he might harbor. For when she arrived at police headquarters she learned that the good detective had called in sick that morning.

"A bad case of poison ivy," Officer Bolduc informed her.

"Poison sumac," she corrected him, but doubted that the young man heard what she said, barricaded as he was behind a glass partition, with only a small aperture—reminiscent of the peephole in a Prohibition-era speakeasy—through which to communicate.

Dedicated public servant that he was, Detective Armenian had left instructions with a fellow officer to take Lena's statement regarding her discovery of the lunch bag, so that her trip into town was not wasted. Whatever suspicions the detective might foster, her conscience was clear; she had done her civic duty, and could now turn her attention to other things.

Such as avenging Brian's death, an objective best accomplished by discovering the identify of his murderer, and by bringing that person to speedy justice.

When she arrived at the house she found a note from Cheryl on the kitchen table informing her that her friend had at the last moment decided to go shopping at the Independence Mall in Kingston and would not be home for lunch.

And would not, therefore, be on hand to chide Lena for what she was about to do.

⌒ ⌒

She had to try several times, but finally she reached Wompi on his cell phone.

"Lena!" he exclaimed upon hearing her voice. "Where've you been hiding yourself? The last time you phoned you'd just sprained your ankle and were, in your own words, 'bored beyond tears.' You haven't sprained your other ankle, have you? How's Marmalade?"

After a few pleasantries, such as inquiring after her friend's health and apologizing for not keeping in touch, Lena got down to business.

"Wompi, I need your advice. A friend of mine has been murdered."

Wompi Mukquosham aka White Wolf aka Joseph Mitchell maintained absolute silence as Lena related the story of Brian Siminski's death and the circumstances surrounding it.

When she reached the part about the kettle hole and her hunch concerning it, he asked: "When did this strong feeling that the young man's body must lie within the pond first come to you? As soon as you came upon the lunch bag and the rotting apple? Or afterwards?"

"Afterwards. As I stood by the edge of the kettle hole, half daydreaming, a cloud passed overhead and cast its shadow against the surface of the pond. In spite of the summer heat I felt a sudden shiver, as if icy fingers had passed up and down my spine." She paused. "I know all this must sound melodramatic, Wompi, but that's how it was. It was precisely then that I had an image—a vision—of the body lying beneath the surface. Actually, it was the silhouette of a corpse that I saw in my mind's eye."

"A silhouette?" Wompi repeated. "As if cut with scissors from the shadow of the cloud?"

"Why, yes!" Lena exclaimed. "At the time I didn't think of it in those terms. But now that you bring it up that's exactly how I would describe what I saw, or rather, imagined that I saw. The cutout of a man's body."

"It is a sign," Wompi said. "You have been granted a vision. Her spirit is strong within you," he added.

The spirit he referred to was that of an Algonquin ancestor of Lena's, a grandmother many generations remote, whose eternal essence they both, from previous experiences, had come to believe resided within her.

"The question is, how do I persuade the police that my hunch is right?" Lena asked.

"Produce the body," Wompi replied.

CHAPTER XXIII
Old Corpsey

With the abandon of a broncobuster giving free rein to a mustang, Lena jounced the pickup along the dirt track that skirted her bog. Heedless of loose stones the size of grapefruits and the deep ruts that scarred the road—hazards, both, to tailpipe and tires alike—she pressed her foot hard against the gas pedal, spewing a cloud of dust in her wake voluminous enough to catch the attention of fire spotters in towers as far away as Plymouth.

"Whoa," Cheryl protested from the passenger side of the cab. "That last jolt almost sent me through the roof. What's got into you, Lena?"

"Sorry, dear." Lena glanced at her companion with a twisted smile. "I can't help myself. It's so much fun making the police eat dust! And don't you just love the way the Canada geese swoop off in a panic? It serves the pests right, given all the damage they do to the vines." She heaved a sigh. "I suppose I should slow down, else Officer Mills will be handing me a ticket for speeding on my own property."

She eased her foot from the accelerator and glanced at the rearview mirror. "I can't see a thing with all this dust, but I think she's way behind. Perhaps blinded by the dust she swerved into a ditch. I hope not. I'd never forgive myself," she added with a chuckle. She slowed even more. "I'll give her a chance to catch up. She knows the way to the screenhouse, of course, but I don't want her to think I'm showing off. It wouldn't do to antagonize her too much at this stage. We may be in need of her help."

"What exactly for? You're being very mysterious, Lena," her friend complained.

"I'm not quite sure myself, dear. Wompi gave me a phone number to call, which I did. The woman who answered was rather abrupt, in fact quite rude, until I mentioned Wompi's name. After that she was less rude, though not what you would call cordial. But I suppose we have to take people as they come. She's agreed to help me out; that's what's important."

"Help you find Eric Russell's body," Cheryl said.

"Yes, dear."

"Assuming he's dead."

"Yes, dear."

"But how?"

"That I can't say. As I said, she was rather abrupt."

"She may not even show up."

"Oh, she'll show up, dear. Wompi assured me that she's thoroughly reliable."

"And how much is this person charging you for her so-called assistance?" Cheryl, ever the skeptic, asked.

"Why, nothing. When I asked her what the cost would be, she let me know in no uncertain terms that she's helping me out solely because I'm a friend of Wompi's. Did I mention that she's a Mashpee Indian?"

"You did not."

"Though himself not a member of the Mashpee tribe, Wompi holds a high position among the Wampanoags and is greatly respected."

Arrived at the screenhouse, Lena nosed the pickup up to the edge of the swamp. The two women climbed out of the cab and stood waiting for Officer Mills to arrive. When, moments later, the cruiser pulled up next to them it was coated in road dust, looking like a breakfast cruller powdered with confectioners' sugar. Officer Mills looked none too happy when she exited the vehicle. She glared at Lena with baleful eyes but said nothing.

Lena would have preferred that Detective Armenian be present, but that esteemed officer of the law was still indisposed from exposure to the poison sumac with which he had rashly (Lena could not suppress the pun) allowed himself to come in contact. He had assigned Officer Mills in his stead. Though Mills was too much of a professional to voice her sentiments, it was obvious from her demeanor that she was not overly pleased with the assignment, which, along with her superior, she doubtlessly believed to be a waste of time.

"We're a few minutes early," Lena remarked. "She should be arriving shortly."

"Does this 'she' for whom we're waiting have a name?" Cheryl asked. She herself had agreed to tag along only at the last moment—and only because Lena, with her oblique hints and cryptic remarks, had piqued the younger woman's curiosity.

"Her name is Pearl Starbuck. Whether Miss, Mrs., or Ms. I can't say. 'You can call me Pearl,' she snapped at me when, on the phone, I addressed her as Ms. Starbuck."

"She sounds like a dragon," Cheryl said.

"We'll find out soon enough. Here she comes now," Lena said.

The dilapidated Dodge pickup that lurched to a stop two feet shy of where the threesome stood made Lena's battered Ford look like a Rolls Royce in comparison. Once a fiery red, it had, where not scratched, scraped, dinged or dented, bled to an anemic pink. Bare of all tread, the tires were as shiny as a hobo's heels.

Officer Mills glanced at the vehicle's inspection sticker as if doubting its currency. Apparently all was in order, for she said nothing, though from the dour look on her face she seemed sorely tempted to condemn the pickup then and there.

Contrary to Cheryl's expectations, it was an actual woman and not a fire-breathing dragon who slid out of the cab. She was no fashion queen, however. Outfitted for business—assuming that that business was the locating of dead bodies—she had on a man's short-sleeved shirt loosely tucked into the waistband of dungaree cutoffs. The cutoffs, tattered and frizzy at the ends, though admittedly clean, were as anemic as the pickup, the fabric, worn thin, having faded to the washed-out blue the sky becomes in early autumn when streaked with high thin clouds. Soft-leather moccasins, fashioned by herself?

or by some other tribal member? completed her attire.

Without a word of greeting or even a cursory nod to acknowledge the presence of others she hopped into the back of the pickup. Squeezing into the space next to an aluminum skiff, she began rummaging through an assortment of boxes and crates.

Lena took the opportunity to examine her closely.

Pearl Starbuck was short, about five feet two, and wiry, her tawny complexion peppered with freckles—giving the impression, to Lena at least, that she had spent the greater portion of her life outdoors. Her callused hands lent credence to the supposition. A lifetime spent on the waters of Buzzards Bay or Nantucket Sound? Or, less romantically, on some golf course? As groundskeeper? Or club member? Outdoors, though, most decidedly: exposed to wind and sun and the exigencies of Cape Cod's variable climate.

She appeared to be in her late twenties or early thirties. She wore her straight black hair short; and yet, despite all this—the abrupt mannerisms, the casual attire, the cropped hair—she was not unattractive, exuded in fact an aura of assured femininity, as if she was well aware of her own worth as an object of desire to the opposite sex.

Lena moved up to the side of the pickup and introduced herself. "I'm Lena Lombardi," she said with a welcoming smile.

Without glancing up Pearl continued to sort through the crates and boxes. She did, however, manage a grunt, which Lena took as an acknowledgment of her greeting.

Officer Mills drifted over. Perhaps she felt bored, or left out of things. Cheryl, feeling lazy, found a shady spot under a towering pine, where she patted down a mass of last year's fallen needles to make a comfortable cushion for herself, and there awaited developments.

"Pearl is going to help us find Eric Russell's body, assuming it's in there," Lena, nodding toward the swamp in the general direction of the kettle hole, explained to Officer Mills.

Pearl Starbuck spoke for the first time. "I ain't. It might." She pointed to a crate wedged next to the skiff's bow.

Officer Mills cocked a dubious eye at the crate. "If that's a dog you've got in there you're wasting our time."

Pearl unlatched the crate. "Stick your head in there and see if it's a dog."

Lena could not suppress a chuckle. She was beginning to like this Pearl Starbuck, this no-nonsense gal who, like herself, did not suffer fools gladly, and who, obviously, was not intimidated by someone just because that person wore the emblems of authority.

Scowling, Officer Mills kept silent as Pearl, scrunched on her knees, peered into the crate. Satisfied, apparently, by what she saw, the young woman thrust her hand inside and dragged out a snapping turtle. She held on to the reptile precariously by its stubby tail as, taking her time, she straightened her body and regained her footing. Twisting its neck, the reptile strained to bring its powerful jaws within range of Pearl's arm and raked its feet wildly at the air, as if to claw the very eyes from the sky, all the while hissing like a fiend fresh from the depths of Hell.

Officer Mills's own, mammalian, jaw dropped in astonished awe. Lena, too, was taken aback.

Cheryl hurried over to see what the commotion was about. Seeing the reptile, she gasped, and immediately backed off, to remain at a prudent distance. Having spent her childhood in southeastern Massachusetts, she was no stranger to snapping turtles; she knew the damage they could do, how, in a trice, they could lop off a finger or seize a chunk of living flesh from the careless or unwary.

This fellow was an especially big specimen, the grandfather of all snappers. From tip of tail to snout it must have measured a good thirty-six inches or more. Holding the turtle out at arm's length as if it were a severed head, Pearl pivoted to the side of the truck where, though aghast, Officer Mills held her ground.

"You take him whilst I untie the boat."

Mills yanked her head back just in time to save her nose from amputation.

"Keep that thing away from me! You're supposed to help us find Eric Russell's body, not mutilate mine."

Pearl turned to Lena. "Here, you take old Corpse Finder. Or are you scared, too?" She dangled the turtle over the sideboard.

Rather than take offense, Lena cracked a smile. She appreciated

Pearl for assuming she might be equal to the task, for her lack of deference for Lena's advanced years.

Stretching her arm upward she said: "If you'll just lower your friend an inch or two I'll grab hold of its tail."

Lena had handled snappers before. Had, in her salad days, captured them in the wild, beheaded, gutted, cooked, and consumed them. According to the old-time Swamp Yankees she had known in her youth, snappers contained seven types of meat, one that tasted like chicken, another like pork, etc. They certainly were excellent in soups and stews, roasted, or grilled on a skewer like shish kabob.

Now, however, grown wiser and more conservation-minded, whenever she came across one on her property she let it be; she even helped protect their cached eggs from predators such as raccoons, by digging in the sand and erecting wire cages around the eggs. Whenever she encountered one on a paved road attempting to cross to the other side, she stopped her vehicle to protect the creature from oncoming traffic.

True, snappers were notorious for taking their toll on waterfowl, ducks and goslings, in ponds and streams seizing their legs from beneath and pulling the young birds under. But a creature that helped rid the cranberry bogs of pesky Canada geese deserved praise, not censure.

Too bad they didn't eat muskrats.

Or who knows? Perhaps they did. All the more reason to revere these antediluvian reptiles.

The transfer proved tricky. Lena's fingers were not as nimble as they once had been; she nearly let the stubby tail slip through her grasp, but at the last moment was able to squeeze tight and hang on. Just how long she could continue to do so was another matter. The damn thing was heavy, and wouldn't keep still.

Seeing her difficulty Pearl said: "If you hold onto old Corpsey till I can get this skiff off the truck I'd be obliged."

"It smells awful," Cheryl remarked, wrinkling her nose.

Officer Mills looked skeptical. "That thing will locate a body?"

"Uh huh," Pearl grunted. Jumping to the ground, she lowered the tailgate and seizing the bow dragged the aluminum boat toward her. "Take hold of one side," she commanded.

Officer Mills glowered but did as instructed. Together they lowered the skiff onto the ground.

Pearl hoisted herself into the bed of the pickup, grabbed an oak dowel from a heap of trash, along with a length of nylon cord, and hopped down beside Lena. With the dowel she rapped old Corpse Finder on the head, none too gently. "To get his attention," she explained. The snapper clamped its jaws onto the wood. Had it been a broom handle it would have snapped in two. "That'll keep him occupied." She took hold of the dowel and swung it, along with the clinging turtle, into the skiff.

"You've got that down to a science," Lena said in admiration.

"Do you mind telling me exactly how that thing is going to locate a body?" Officer Mills demanded.

"Snappers love carrion," Pearl said. "It's caviar to them. If there's rotten meat in that kettle hole Old Corpsey will sniff it out."

Officer Mills sniffed (surely not deliberately?) with disdain. But regardless of what she might be thinking of Pearl's, and the snapper's, body-finding capabilities, she kept a discreet silence.

Pearl unraveled the cord and threaded the end through a grommet that had been drilled into one of the snapper's serrated plates, just above its tail. She secured the cord with a knot so that the turtle was, in effect, on a leash.

"Do you plan on walking him in?" Officer Mills asked, innocently enough, though Lena thought she detected an undercurrent of sarcasm.

"You and I are going to carry him in," Pearl said. She wrapped the loose end of the cord around the seat in the midsection of the skiff, leaving enough slack in the cord so that the turtle could move about the bottom of the boat but not crawl over the side. Turning to Lena she asked: "Where's that kettle hole?"

It was a good thing, Lena reflected, that she had already blazed a trail through the swamp to the kettle hole, and that the repeated passage of bodies—hers, Cheryl's, and Detective Armenian's—had flattened the vegetation and otherwise helped widen the pathway. Even so, it was not an easy portage; only with great difficulty was Pearl, with the reluctant assistance of Officer Mills, able to transport the skiff (fabricated of lightweight aluminum, fortunately, and not of ponderous wood) and its reptilian passenger to its aqueous destination.

Under ordinary circumstances two people might easily have borne the boat along, each holding on to a side with one hand, ready to launch it with a gentle shove. Lena's makeshift trail, alas, did not allow for that; it was far too narrow. The constricted pathway necessitated that one person be at the bow, the other at the stern, the former position being the more arduous; the person there had, in effect, to walk backwards much of the time.

Pearl, rough exterior notwithstanding, exhibited her sporting nature by assigning Officer Mills the stern position. "Just be careful where you put your hands," she admonished. "Old Corpsey would like nothing better than to sample one of your fingers as an hors d'oeuvre."

Lena, familiar with the way, took the vanguard, urging the others on whenever they faltered. Cheryl took up the rear. To her great surprise the petite professor of English literature found that she was actually enjoying herself. The role of mere looker on in one of Lena's madcap adventures was a welcome change from that of active participant.

The only member of the party not enjoying herself was Officer Mills.

At long last, after much exertion, some of it verbal—especially on the part of Officer Mills (such language, so unbecoming to a lady!)—they reached their destination. The yellow crime-scene tape, one end of which Detective Armenian had, unwittingly, secured to a poison sumac bush, was still in place, marking the spot where Lena had come upon the remnant of Eric Russell's lunch-bag-cum-apple.

The lunch bag...

That pathetic scrap of paper, scribbled with the letters of a partial name, seemed suddenly to Lena insufficient reason for the four of them being there. Pearl Starbuck driving up all the way from the Cape, the absurdity of the snapping turtle, Officer Mills's sullen acquiescence, the fatiguing trek through the swamp: all for what? For naught?

No wonder Cheryl wore an amused look on her face. She, if no one else, could fully appreciate the farce which the four of them were enacting.

"This looks like as good a place as any," Pearl agreed when, arrived at the kettle hole, Lena directed her to a spot at the edge free of overhanging brush. She lowered the bow of the skiff in such a way that it faced the water.

"Still got all your fingers?" she said to Officer Mills. Then added: "I wouldn't get too close to that bush if I was you. It's poison sumac. Who's the damn fool that tied that yellow tape to it?"

Seizing the painter coiled at the base of the bow, she handed the loose end to Cheryl. "Hold onto this so's the boat don't drift off. I ain't in the mood for swimming after it." Nudging Officer Mills away from the stern she shoved the boat halfway into the water, then climbed inside and unlooped the cord that was attached at one end to Old Corpse Finder from around the seat. Giving the snapper as wide a berth as the confines of the skiff allowed, she clambered across to the bow.

"I'll need a helper," she announced. "Someone to row. Any volunteers?" She glanced toward Officer Mills.

"I'm not getting into that boat," Mills declared. "Not with that hideous thing crawling underfoot."

"I haven't rowed for quite some time, but I'd like to give it a try," Cheryl said.

"Are you sure, dear?" Lena asked, with a pang of conscience. "This whole thing is my idea; why should you be the one to put yourself in harm's way? Let me do the rowing."

"Oh, but I want to," Cheryl protested. She was about to add, "I haven't had this much fun since the pigs ate my baby brother," but thought better of it. This was, after all, a solemn occasion, no time for levity. One young man murdered, another, his friend, missing…even if they were successful in their mission and discovered Eric Russell's remains, there would be no cause for celebration. Herself a mother, she thought of poor Mrs. Russell, for whom as yet there might still be a glimmer of hope, but for whom, in all probability, only grief and sorrow lay ahead.

"I left the life jackets back at the truck," Pearl said. "I can fetch one for you if you want me to."

"Don't bother," Cheryl said. "I'm a good swimmer. Besides, you don't look like the type who would capsize a boat."

"You don't, neither," Pearl said, affably. "If you ain't afraid of old Corpse Finder biting off your toes let's get a move on."

Cheryl got into the boat, taking her place in the center. Pearl had already tugged the turtle close to herself; she kept it there, ready with the dowel "in case he forgets his manners."

With a nod from Pearl, Officer Mills shoved them off.

Following Pearl's instructions Cheryl grabbed the oars and rowed toward the center of the pond. To her own amazement she found that she retained her nautical skills and was able to row with ease. In less than five minutes they were at the center of the kettle hole. With no breeze blowing the boat remained there, more or less stationary, needing only an occasional nudge with an oar blade to keep it in place.

The water was nearly crystal clear, though tannin leached from fallen leaves gave it a brownish tinge. Insects skimmed along the surface. On the side of the pond opposite from where Lena and Officer Mills stood watching, Cheryl spotted a kingfisher perched low on an overhanging maple bough.

For a moment she was able to forget their reason for being there, the tranquillity of the scene so belied the bloated horror which, if Lena's hunch were true, lay beneath the surface. But only for a moment…

Nonchalantly, as if retrieving a picnic basket, Pearl yanked on the nylon cord to which the snapping turtle was attached, and drew the reptile, dangling upside down, from the bottom of the boat.

"Watch your knees," she said as lifting the turtle higher she swung her arm like a boom over the side, and letting go of the cord, sent the creature flying.

The snapper hit the surface with a broad splash that sent water droplets into the boat and onto its occupants. As if indifferent to the antics of the human race, the kingfisher maintained its perch on the maple bough. Immediately the snapper sank beneath the ripples, where for the course of a few seconds it remained as if stunned, its carapace like the hulk of a sunken vessel barely discernible, until following some chelonian instinct it struck out, away from the skiff, trailing the cord behind it.

"Old Corpsey ain't been fed for a week," Pearl said. "If there's a cadaver in there he'll find it."

For the next ten minutes, the sun a fiery ball overhead, like sailors adrift in a lifeboat they floated. *On a Sargasso Sea of expectation,* Cheryl reflected ruefully. What madness was this anyhow, two women alone in an aluminum boat, seeking a corpse with the aid of a snapping turtle? The water which the turtle had splashed onto her rapidly dried, to be replaced by beads of perspiration. At the rim of the pond, silently observing, Lena and Officer Mills stood like marooned mariners helpless to assist their becalmed comrades. Cheryl and Pearl might have spoken, one to the other or, by shouting, to those on the shore, but they too chose silence.

Slowly, like a compass needle seeking North, the skiff, drawn by the cord tautened by the turtle, swung in a semicircle.

Pearl pointed to an imaginary spot a few degrees to the left of where Lena and the officer were standing. "Row that-away," she said.

Cheryl did as instructed. As they neared the spot the cord slackened.

"We'd best hurry," Pearl said.

Why? Cheryl wondered. Then shuddered at the obvious answer.

Pearl began to haul in the cord, coiling the slack at her feet. Three or four yards off shore, and a dozen feet from where they had launched the skiff, she called a halt.

"If you'll just hold her steady I'll pull in the rest of this here slack. Oops. Old Corpsey's tugging away something fierce; he don't wanna be deprived of his dinner. Don't worry, you old rascal," she shouted, in encouragement to the still submerged snapper. "I won't let you go hungry." Seeing Cheryl's appalled expression, she hastily explained: "I got a tub full of rotten fish on the truck. For the ride home I'll toss Corpsey into it, so's he can dine in style. By the time I get him back to Mashpee he'll stink to high heaven. But then, he don't smell all that nice to begin with.

"Ups-a-daisy!" she said, as she yanked the recalcitrant reptile into the skiff.

After securing it, hissing, to the seat, she took hold of a gaff that Cheryl had seen lying at the bottom of the boat but to which until now she had paid scant attention. With a sinking feeling in the pit of her stomach she suddenly understood its purpose.

"This won't take but a minute," Pearl said. "If you don't wanna look you can turn your head. I won't take nothing into the boat. I just want to make sure it's what we've been looking for. If it is, we'll let the police handle the rest."

Leaning over the side, she began to probe.

CHAPTER XXIV
Connections

The gazebo comfortably seated four, leaving sufficient, if not ample, room for the plump Marmalade, who lay cozily ensconced beneath the table between opposing pairs of feet, the only hazard to his comfort and well-being that of his tail being pinched by an errant shoe.

The four humans were eating blueberry pie, which Lena had baked that very morning, having felt the need "to do something with my hands, something to take my mind off of those two unfortunate young men."

"I've never had such good pie," Officer Mills confessed. "I grew up in Boston; my mom was a good cook, but she didn't like to bake. Besides, where would she have gotten wild high bush blueberries? They don't grow on the streets of Roxbury."

"Please have another piece," Lena insisted. "You've only had two so far, and the second was just a sliver. I baked four pies this morning, can you believe it?" She turned to Detective Armenian. "You, too, Detective. Come on now. The antioxidants in the blueberries will do your rash from the poison sumac a world of good." She didn't know if that was true, but surely they could do the rash no harm.

Poor man. He looked so uncomfortable, as if he itched all over. As no doubt he did. She recalled their outward trek from the swamp, after he had inadvertently handled the poison sumac bush. He had at one point excused himself and sought out a thicket, behind which he presumably answered a call from nature. Oh dear! Having touched himself *there*, with oil of sumac all over his hands, no wonder he felt miserable.

Detective Armenian hesitated. "Well, just a small piece." He patted his paunch. "I have to admit I've never eaten native wild blueberries before. Just the low bush variety from Maine."

"These high bush berries are plumper," Lena said. She cut a generous slice and handed it over. "Plump and juicy."

"More iced coffee?" Cheryl inquired. Without waiting for a response she lifted the pitcher and topped off everyone's glass.

Detective Armenian, sighing with contentment, helped himself to more cream. The lotion he'd applied to his face and hands that morning had dried to a flaky paste, so that he resembled a pastry chef who, having labored for hours in a hot kitchen, has finally paused for a much-needed break.

A minute or two went by in which nobody spoke. It was by no means an awkward silence; everyone was just too busy eating to bother with conversation.

It was Lena who broke the silence. "Now Detective, in all honesty, do I look like a homicidal maniac?"

Detective Armenian pretended to scrutinize her closely. "Is that why you asked Officer Mills and I to pay this little visit? So that you can confess?"

That, Lena reflected, *should be "Officer Mills and* me." *"Me" is the object of the verb "asked."* Lena was, of course, too polite to correct his grammar. Cheryl, the English professor, seemed never to be bothered by others' lapses in grammar, probably because having for years taught today's semiliterate high school grads she had grown inured.

"It was good of you and Officer Mills to come," Lena said.

"Ah, but we would have come anyhow, even if you hadn't asked us to. Or I would have invited you and Professor Fernandes to meet us at headquarters."

"In which case you would have missed out on Lena's blueberry pie," Cheryl pointed out.

"True," the detective admitted. "In all seriousness, though," he added, shifting his gaze from Cheryl to Lena, "why is it you wanted to see me?"

By way of reply Lena countered with a question of her own: "Was Eric Russell murdered?"

The detective thought awhile, then shrugged. "I can't see any harm in telling you what will be made public soon enough: yes, the autopsy showed that he was killed by a blow with a blunt instrument to the back of his head."

"I knew he must have been murdered," Lena said. "The theory that he somehow, deliberately or accidentally, killed Brian Siminski, then, out of remorse, took his own life made no sense. No sense whatsoever."

"So what sense do you make of the situation?" Detective Armenian asked.

Oh, he's a coy one, Lena thought. *String the old lady along, see if maybe she doesn't stumble. Well, she could hardly blame him. She was acting a bit peculiar.*

"I have a hunch." Seeing the expression on his face she hastily added: "Now, before you make disparaging remarks, please remember that it was my so-called 'intuition' that led to the discovery of Eric Russell's body in the kettle hole."

"So it was," Detective Armenian agreed. Perhaps too readily?

"Well then," Lena said. "I've been piecing together bits of information, facts that I've gleaned from Brian's aunt, Phyllis Baker, and from Elizabeth Walderne, the cranberry grower who lives here in town. And Cheryl here"—she nodded toward her friend—"has been digging, at my request, through old newspaper files at the library." She took a sip of iced coffee. Hmm. Not wine, but not bad, either. But would the caffeine keep her awake all night?

"And...?" the detective asked.

"And, I think there's a connection between these two killings and the murder, ten years ago, of Amanda Verfurth."

Disappointment ran on little feet across the detective's face. "How can you possibly believe that?" he asked. He might have added, *we already have a suspect in that case, the husband, Kurt Verfurth. These two murdered young men were probably involved with drugs; that seems to account for most crime these days. That is, unless you had your own reasons for wanting the two of them dead.*

"In your questioning of the friends and relatives of Brian and Eric you no doubt learned about the terrible accident that both boys were in some years ago," Lena said. "The accident in which Brian Siminski's brother Brad and another boy, Jacob Britto, were killed, and which left Eric Russell disfigured and, well, somewhat damaged mentally."

Detective Armenian nodded. "Eric's mother told Officer Mills and me all about it. The poor woman was so distraught she told us all sorts of irrelevant stories about her son; out of compassion I let her go on."

"Her son was her whole life," Officer Mills said. "I'd like to see whoever killed him brought to justice."

"I still don't see..." Detective Armenian said.

Lena finished the sentence for him. "Any possible connection with Amanda Verfurth's murder."

"Exactly."

"Speaking of exactitude: Do you know exactly when the accident occurred?"

"No. Why would I?"

I won't touch that one, Lena reflected. *Far be it from me to tell you how to conduct your investigations. Though, come to think of it, that's precisely what I'm about to do.* "It occurred ten years ago, on a Saturday night. The same Saturday on which Amanda Verfurth was last seen alive."

"That's interesting," the detective said. "But surely nothing more than coincidence."

"The two boys were murdered shortly after her remains were discovered."

"Now that means nothing. Absolutely nothing." Absently, he reached down beneath the table top.

Oh, don't scratch yourself there, Lena thought to herself. *You're bound to regret it!*

"Maybe so," she said. "But Brad Siminski had worked one or two summers for Amanda's neighbors, the Waldernes." *She was forgetting that Elizabeth's husband's last name was not Walderne, but Cardozo. No matter.* "Their bogs border some of the Verfurth bogs. Including the

149

one in which her skeleton was found."

"All of this is lost on me," Detective Armenian said. "What is it you're implying?"

"Bear with me," Lena said. "More pie?"

He shook his head. "Thank you, but no. I'm filled to the gills as it is."

"Officer Mills?"

"No thank you, Mrs. Lombardi. Even though it's the best pie I've ever eaten."

Cheryl said, "Don't look at me. I've had my pie quota for the week."

"The boys were drinking that night," Lena went on, returning to her summary. "There were five of them. The name of the fifth is Jay O'Sullivan. He, by the way, was twenty-one, the only one of legal age. The others were all minors. It was probably Jay who supplied the alcohol—though of course there's no proof of that, and at this late date it hardly matters."

"I've questioned O'Sullivan," Detective Armenian said. "As a matter of course, since he was an acquaintance of the slain men. He never mentioned the accident. But then, why would he?"

"I think he was the driver that night," Lena said. "But that, too, is supposition. And not relevant to my theory."

"Which is…?" the detective asked, in the tone of voice of one who is losing patience.

"Well, maybe 'theory' is too strong a word," Lena replied. "For now I'll stick to 'hunch.'" *Or better yet, wild guess.* "I'm getting to it. I want first to lay everything on the table, as it were, so that you can see things the way I do." She brushed at a fly which, having somehow found its way into the screened-in enclosure, was buzzing around the cream pitcher.

"Shortly before he was murdered Brian did a job for the Waldernes, between the time he finished repairing my pump house and the time he got started on the screenhouse. And—this you can accept or dismiss as nonsense—there was something odd, for lack of a better word, between Brian and the Waldernes. Something strained. A tension of sorts. That, at least, is my impression."

"Can you be more specific?" Detective Armenian asked.

Lena shook her head. "No," she stated flatly.

The fly had lighted on the pie pan and was wading in the gooey purple liquid at the bottom. No real harm done; there was only the tiniest sliver of pie remaining anyhow. Did Detective Armenian regard her, with her wild surmises, as a pest, like the fly, Lena wondered—or did he in truth consider her to be a suspect? If so, the man was a fool. Like the fly, mired in his own stupidity.

"Next?" the detective asked.

"There is no next," Lena said. "Those are the facts."

"And the conjectures."

"Yes," she conceded.

He nodded. And then surprised her by saying, "You know, there may be something to your 'theory.'"

Lena, though pleased—the man was finally showing some intelligence—said: "But you haven't heard it yet."

He shrugged. "Let me see if I can guess. The woods around secluded cranberry bogs have always been, and continue to be, ideal locations for underage binge drinking. Brian's brother Brad, one of the two boys who were killed in the automobile accident, from having worked there was familiar with the layout around both the Walderne bogs and the adjacent Verfurth bogs. On that fatal Saturday night when they had their little booze party they saw something. Maybe not the act of murder itself, but someone in the area acting suspicious."

"Or," Officer Mills interjected, "they were themselves seen."

"Good point," the detective said. "Were seen by the killer and recognized." He paused. "Then what?"

Officer Mills thought for a moment. "The boys were intoxicated. Kids that age can't handle alcohol. They drink too much and too fast. Did they even know they'd been seen?"

"For any of this to make sense," Cheryl said—having until now maintained a discreet silence—"they'd have to know they'd been seen. Unless it was they who did the seeing and then confronted the killer. What I mean is, there had to have been mutual knowledge, recognition, between them and the killer."

"If the boys saw something that night, why didn't they come forward with the knowledge?" Detective Armenian wondered aloud.

"There was the accident," Officer Mills reminded him. "Brad and Jacob killed, Eric seriously injured—his memory erased. That leaves Brian and Jay. Did they even know they'd seen something. Something relevant? They were drinking in the woods and saw and were seen by someone they knew. So what. Not until Amanda Verfurth was reported missing might they have attached any significance to the incident. By then they were suffering from their own guilt. It would be easy at that point to dismiss whatever they saw as being of no importance."

"The question remains: who?" Cheryl said. "Who saw them, whom did they see, and was this 'who' the same person who killed Amanda, and, ten years later, Brian and Eric?"

"There's another possibility," Officer Mills said, barely suppressing her excitement. "Suppose it was the boys who committed the murder! They're out in the woods drinking. Somehow they encounter Amanda. It's a lovely spring evening, she's out for a walk. Or on her way home from a tryst. Or she hears a ruckus and foolishly confronts them to order them from her property. They don't intend to kill her—but something happens, things get out of hand. Maybe only one of them is responsible for the deed. In any case suddenly she's dead. In a panic they bury her on the bog, all the while continuing to consume alcohol to bolster their courage. On the way home they crash the car."

Cheryl picked up the scenario: "The two survivors—Eric doesn't count, after the accident he can't remember anything of what happened that night, or if he does remember he's easily convinced it was all a bad dream—the two survivors, Brian Siminski and Jay O'Sullivan, hide their dark secret for ten years. Until…"

"Until," Officer Mills broke in, "a skeleton is unearthed. There's nothing, absolutely nothing, to connect them with the crime. But one of them—Brian—has a conscience. He knows full well that all along Amanda's husband, Kurt Verfuth, has been the prime suspect in his wife's disappearance. Now, with new evidence—the discovery of her remains on his cranberry bog—it's only a matter of time before he's arrested, put on trial, and quite possibly convicted. The time has arrived, Brian concludes, to step forward and confess."

"But," Cheryl said, "Jay O'Suillivan has other ideas. Confess? Are you crazy? He's not about to go to prison for something that happened ten years ago and was, in his way of thinking, more or less an accident anyhow. With Brian and Eric out of the way he has nothing to fear."

"Why kill Eric?" Detective Armenian asked. Then answered his own question. "Two possible reasons. One, Eric, despite his traumatic brain injury, might eventually say something; two—and I think this is more likely—he saw Jay kill Brian and had to be eliminated as a witness to that second murder."

Officer Mills said: "Eric had to've been killed at the kettle hole. It would be nearly impossible to drag a dead body through the swamp to begin with, and totally impossible to do it without leaving a trace. Eric might have been forced to go there at gun point. But I think he was lured by someone he knew. Jay O'Sullivan."

Detective Armenian nodded in agreement. Then sighed. "We've painted a neat little picture of what might have happened. But in the end it all boils down to guesswork. Kurt Verfurth is still our prime suspect."

"Along with Harvey Cardozo," Lena said. "You've been overlooking him all along."

CHAPTER XXV
Plans and Master Plans

As with any worthwhile endeavor, murder requires careful planning, espcially if the murderer hopes to escape the clutches of the law. The devil is in the details. Jay O'Sullivan had already taken care of detail number one, the purchase of the weapon to be used: Sweet Baby, whose paternity could not be traced back to him.

And detail number two? Good question. He hadn't quite yet figured that one out. But give him time; he'd come up with something.

He had to. And damn soon. Time was running out.

Meanwhile in another town, another county, Lena Lombardi was busy formulating plans of her own. Not for murder, of course (though she was perfectly capable of murder, if it came down to that), but for the apprehension of a murderer.

Unlike Jay O'Sullivan, who had no friends, only acquaintances, not one of whom could by the wildest stretch of the imagination be characterized as trustworthy, Lena had as her close confidant Cheryl Fernandes, whose sound judgment Lena considered equal to her own, or nearly so, especially in matters pertaining to minor infractions of the law.

"But what makes you so sure that Harvey Cardozo is our murderer?" Cheryl asked.

The two women were seated in the library. Marmalade, sated with a surfeit of steamed clams and too lazy to bestir himself, had elected to remain in the kitchen, under the table. It was in the early evening of the day following the brainstorming session that had taken place in the gazebo, to which Detective Armenian and Officer Mills had, contrary to Lena's expectations, so generously contributed.

The clams, of which Marmalade had consumed a vast quantity disproportionate to his size, were the gift of Cheryl's paramour, Anthony Gomes, dug by himself that morning on the shores of Buzzard's Bay. Cheryl steamed them in a broth consisting of a pint of Cape Cod Beer's finest India Pale Ale; half a white onion, chopped; and a clove, finely minced, of fresh garlic. If she had had any misgivings regarding Marmalade's tolerance of the latter three ingredients, she need not have concerned herself. *Au contraire.* Perhaps it was the pungent ale—surely not the onion or garlic?—that caused him to overindulge in the savory bivalves to the point of near prostration.

"Call it, if you will, a hunch," Lena replied.

Cheryl groaned audibly.

"Now dear, you have to admit that my hunch about poor Eric being submerged in the kettle hole was right on the button."

"True," her friend conceded. "But in that instance you had solid evidence to go by: the lunch bag with Eric's name on it and his uneaten apple. What evidence do you have of Harvey's guilt?"

"Circumstantial evidence, dear. The fact that Amanda and Harvey were neighbors, owning bogs adjacent to one another (including the one on which her remains were found), within walking distance of each other's house. The fact of Amanda's known proclivity for extramarital affairs. The fact of "Handsome Harvey" being married to a dowdy woman ten years his senior. And Amanda being considerably younger—and physically more attractive—than her husband, Kurt Verfurth. It's science. Simple science."

"Science?"

"Chemistry, dear. The oldest kind. Between man and woman."

"But Detective What's-his-name seems to think Amanda's husband is the killer. Speaking of whom—I mean the detective—I still can't get over how much he confided in us yesterday. And Officer Mills as well."

"Blueberry pie does loosen the tongue," Lena said. "As for Kurt Verfurth, he's obviously the default suspect; they can't find evidence against anyone else so they assume he must be the guilty one."

"And you don't."

"No."

"You suspect the neighbor. But you can't explain why."

"It's the murder of those two boys—Brian and Eric."

"We don't even know for sure that their deaths are connected with Amanda's."

"We keep coming back to that, don't we dear. We keep coming around in circles. But until I have reason to believe otherwise, I'll continue to assume that the three murders are connected. And I'll do everything in my power to find out who's responsible. With your help, of course."

"Now Lena…"

"Don't worry, there shouldn't be too much danger in what I have in mind. At least, I don't think there will be. Though when dealing with a blood-thirsty killer you never know, do you? We'll go armed, of course—that will afford us some protection."

"*You'll* go armed. I won't. In fact, I won't go at all, armed or otherwise."

"Come, come dear. You haven't even heard my plan, and already you're backing out."

"How can I back out of something I never got into in the first place? Lena, you're impossible!"

"Oh, but you must admit that I make your life interesting. Without me to liven things up you'd just be a staid middle-aged English professor teaching at a local university with a boyfriend you can't quite make up your mind about and a daughter living in Lisbon whom you hardly ever see. Now here's what I have in mind…"

What Lena had in mind is of little consequence to the unfolding of this narrative. Her plan for "getting the goods on Harvey"—a plan unworthy of a child of three, let alone a grandam of seventy-three—

involved the two of them visiting the Walderne-Cardozo homestead under the pretense of Professor Fernandes's research into the folklore of local cranberry bogs. The Walderne bogs being among the most venerable in town, built on swamps mined for bog iron by the Pilgrims and their descendants, Lena naturally thought of Elizabeth and Marguerite as veritable fonts of information. (And didn't they owe her a favor, for having directed them to the cadaver of their beloved Pal?)

Once on the property, while Cheryl held their attention, Lena would sneak off to scout around.

"If there's a clue to be found I'll sniff it out," she declared.

"You're grasping at straws," Cheryl said, mixing the metaphor. "Chasing a chimera. I'll have no part of it."

Jay O'Sullivan, on the other hand—now he was a fellow who had *his* plan all figured out. No grasping at straws, this. His was a master plan. Foolproof to boot.

Step one (previously mentioned): the acquisition of Sweet Baby.

Step two: phone call (from phone booth if he could find one. If not, from stolen cell phone).

Step three: appointment.

Step four: deception.

Step five: ambush.

Step six: get his ass out of there.

Step seven: infanticide (the drowning of Sweet Baby in the blue waters of the Atlantic. Somewhere between Cape Cod and Nantucket perhaps?)

The plan, fail-safe, was brilliant for its simplicity. (The fewer the steps, the better.) Step seven? Risky, maybe—holding onto Sweet Baby until he could ditch her into the drink. But he knew someone with a boat, a small yacht he could hire for a day of deep-sea fishing. So—what could possibly go wrong? Nothing. The deck (card deck, not yacht) was stacked, and he was holding all the cards—with Sweet Baby his ace in the hole.

CHAPTER XXVI
What the Crows Said

Caaw.

    Caaw.

        Caaw.

Only gradually did he become aware of the sound the crows made; it was as if walking along a crowded sidewalk a person might hear, in the distance, sporadic voices, loud voices which had been there all along, but which, because they were so much a part of the background, had gone unnoticed.

    Caaw.

        Caaw.

            Caaw.

The crows sounded as if they were upset. They must be mobbing a hawk, harassing it, making vocal their displeasure at its presence, at its predacious existence, giving the raptor no peace until, defeated by their persistent pestering, it took wing to seek prey elsewhere, a quiet bough where there were no abusive crows, a lofty perch from which to swoop down upon unsuspecting rodents, or pluck from flight passing passerines.

Gradually—his intellect was not, after all, functioning at full capacity—he grew aware that it was not a predator, some hapless hawk or owl, toward which the cawings of the crows were directed, but rather toward himself. The crows were mocking him. *Him.* Kurt Verfurth.

The realization gave him great cause for mirth.

Royally drunk, and at such an early hour; it was no wonder that the crows found him amusing. Crows do laugh, you know, he reminded himself. They are highly intelligent creatures, with a keen sense of humor, and can talk, if only you will listen to them closely. On unsteady legs he aimed himself at a low boulder and plunked himself down on it, a boulder flat and large enough to accommodate his commodious butt, and cupping a hand to one ear pretended to eavesdrop on the crows' conversation.

Caaw.

Look at him! Three sheets to the wind.

Disgraceful, at this hour. Scarcely noon.

Did you see how he staggered? How he lurched from side to side, like a dismasted ship?

Haaw haaw.

Stumblebum.

Caaw. Caaw. Caaw.

Pixilated.

Caaw. Caaw. Caaw.

Drunk as a coot.

Haaw haaw.

Look at him, with his hand cupped to his head like an ear trumpet. Thinks we don't know he's listening.

Caaw. Caaw.

He uncupped his hand and used it to wipe the sweat from his brow. Phew! He was not that drunk. Not so drunk as to hear crows talking. Pretending to do so had just been a conceit, a joke, something to occupy his mind, to help, along with the booze, to drive away those other thoughts, those images, those soundless voices that, increasingly, came unbidden, willy-nilly, that would not go away, even in his dreams. Especially in his dreams.

He left the boulder, and the crows along with it (perhaps they had been mobbing a hawk after all), and continued walking along the dirt track. The walk would do him good. He was not piss-pants drunk, just slightly inebriated. That bit about staggering had been an exaggeration. A fib. A nifty comparison, though: *like a dismasted ship*.

Where was he headed? There was swamp on either side of the

road, bog ahead. He knew where he was, but not where he was going. He hadn't quite made up his mind.

After a few minutes he came to an intersection at which he had a choice of ways. He tarried, assessing his sobriety, or the lack of it. At length he chose to follow the dirt track that swung to the left; though the longest route, it would lead him, eventually, back to his house. Once there he would take a nap. That would kill the afternoon. In the evening, after supper, he would get drunk again.

That would kill the night.

In the meantime, though, there were the thoughts, the images, the face—hers—that plagued him.

Never in his whole life had Kurt Verfurth been a coward; he was not one now. Even so he was afraid. Afraid not of others, but of his thoughts. Of the demons that haunted his mind. He was most afraid of that arch demon, the demon from whom there could be no escape: himself.

As long as Amanda had been merely missing he had been able to cope. When she disappeared—poof! just like that—leaving behind everything she possessed—the gold, the diamonds, the costly trinkets which in his folly he had lavished upon her, or which she had in her own folly lavished (with his money) upon herself; the perfumes, the dresses, the shoes, the lingerie, all the things which her vanity had demanded, and for the sake of which (and for no other reason) she had married him—and in the ensuing weeks, months, years, never reappearing to claim what was hers—and the much more that wasn't hers by right, but which she might have wrested from him—he knew, of course, that she must be dead. Just as he had known, when she agreed to marry him, that she in no way loved, liked, or even respected him.

Notwithstanding the knowledge—that surely she must be dead—as long as she was *merely missing* there had still been a faint flicker of hope. She might just possibly be alive. Suffering from amnesia—absurd, perhaps, but stranger things have been known to happen. Or she may have left on a whim, with a lover who would soon tire of her, or (more likely) of whom she would soon tire, when his youth, or his health, or more likely his money, ran out.

There had been hope.

Just as in the early days of their marriage he had kept alive the hope that, just possibly, she might, somehow, in time come to love him, not as much as he loved her to be sure, but a little bit, or if not love, at least feel fondness for him, a warm affection, just a little, enough to cause her to stay with him, remain his wife.

Slowly that hope had—from her cruel taunts, her many infidelities, her open scorn for him—shriveled and died.

Within his soul hope had died.

But not love. Never love.

Love had, like a quivering thing at the side of the road, broken but alive, lingered on.

Now, that other hope, of the forlorn variety, that pipe dream of his, that she might still be alive; that, with memory restored, or repentant, or just plain desperate, she might some day return; that hearing a knock at the door he would rush to answer it, would wrench it open and find her standing there, teary-eyed, or if not teary-eyed, if not regretful, then defiant—but *there*—that hope had been shattered by the discovery of her…remains. Her skeleton. Her bones.

That he had all along been a prime suspect in her disappearance, and continued to be one in her murder, did not trouble him in the least. What did he care what the police thought? Or anyone? The townspeople, the neighbors, the former so-called friends, all of whom reviled him? The bog workers who showed up each day because he paid them to? What did he care what they thought?

He knew his innocence.

And his guilt.

He was innocent of killing Amanda.

He was guilty of having loved Amanda. Of having married Amanda knowing full well that she did not love him. He was guilty of having hoped that some day Amanda, too, might learn to love.

Him.

Love him.

Kurt Verfurth, the liar, the cheat, the college dropout, the oil field roustabout, the two-bit bozo who, a loser all his life, had, seeing his one main chance, taken that chance and made a fortune smuggling drugs from Mexico, and having made that fortune had, just in the nick of time, just days before the inevitable bust, bailed out, had hightailed it East where he wasn't known, had invested in cranberries of all ridiculous things (up until the day he bought his first bog he labored under the misconception that cranberries grew on trees), had fallen head over heels in love with a two-bit floozy half his age from the faded sea-side resort village of Onset, and in age-old fashion, flaunting his money, had asked (begged) her to marry him, and the rest was history.

⌒⌒

Hell, he needed a drink.

He was sweating profusely, as much from heat and the exertion of walking as from the booze. Thirst scorched his throat like an acetylene torch; at this extremity he would have accepted a drink of anything—including water—had it been offered him.

At some point in his rambles, unnoticed by him, the dirt track had debouched into a clearing, beyond which was an expanse of cranberry bog. He recognized the bog as one of his own—though not, fortunately, the one in which Amanda had lain for ten years under the vines, her flesh, eaten by worms, slowly rotting from her bones.

The sun's rays beating against his head caused it to throb, the pain a forerunner to the fierce hangover he could count on later. On the bog heat waves shimmered above the vines; the odor of moist peat permeated the air, musty but not unpleasant. Across the bog, on the far shore, something moved. A black dog.

Cerberus, come to drag him to Hades?

But didn't Cerberus have three heads? This dog had only one head. (Or perhaps two—but that was only the booze making him see double.)

Pal. No doubt it was Pal, his neighbors', the Waldernes', Lab. Good ol' Pal.

But wait a sec…wasn't Pal dead? Harvey himself had told him that someone across town—a cranberry grower, Lena Lombardi—

162

had found the poor brute's body in the swamp. Pal's replacement then. Ah, sure enough—there were Elizabeth and Marguerite emerging from the woods. Elizabeth probably had to take a pee, the old cow. That's why he hadn't noticed them at first. Seeing him, they waved. He waved back.

Unlike many of his neighbors and fellow growers, the Waldernes, all three of them (Kurt considered Harvey a Walderne, even though his last name was Cardozo), had always treated him decently. Well, they had never, when she was alive, thought highly of Amanda; he had sensed that, on the few occasions when he and Amanda ran into any of them by chance. There had been a tension between her and them. They had, of course, commiserated with him when she went missing. A formality, nothing more, what was expected of neighbors.

Just as—again a formality—he had commiserated with Harvey when Pal went missing and was found dead.

He no doubt felt more badly about Pal's demise than they did about Amanda's.

They had not, however, invited them to the dog's…burial. (You could hardly call it a funeral.) Perhaps they felt awkward. A missing dog, a missing wife. Not exactly an equation.

He hoped the two sisters and their new pooch would not come his way. He felt in no mood, or condition, for small talk. It would be awkward, at the least. What do you say to a man whose missing wife's skeleton has been found buried on a section of his own cranberry bog? They had already offered their condolences. What would they talk about now? The weather? His excessive drinking? How much evidence the police had, or believed they had, against him?

Ah, they were turning down the dirt road that led to their own property. He would be spared any attempts at polite conversation. Though, he supposed, he would have to get acquainted with the new Lab sometime or other. At least learn its name.

Had they seen him staggering? He hoped not. He still had some pride, some vanity.

They might—like that raucous flock of crows—be talking about him at this very moment. Speculating on the motives for his drunkenness, his possible guilt.

Caaw.

Caaw.

Caaw.

Look at him! Did you see how unsteady he was on his feet, lurching from side to side? He's plastered. Again!

Do you think he killed her, Marguerite? Does he drink in order to forget?

Naaw. He wouldn't have the nerve to murder his wife and bury her like that, on his own property. He's a wimp. Do I think he's guilty? Naaw.

Is he lonely? Is that why he drinks?

Don't be a fool, Elizabeth. With his money he doesn't have to be lonely. He can afford to buy companionship.

Money can't buy happiness, Marguerite.

How well I know, sister. How well I know.

Caaw.

Caaw.

Caaw.

Not that he cared, really. What others thought of him was of little consequence. Even so, it was best to keep up appearances. Exactly why that might be important, he couldn't say. Instinct perhaps. Self-preservation.

Rather than heading down the pathway that would lead him directly home, he chose instead to walk around the perimeter of the bog, hoping to clear his head.

God, he was thirsty! Thirsty enough to drink ditch water, almost. A dog would. A dog would drink ditch water. Might even like the taste of it. A dog would wade around in the ditch first. Stir up the mud with its paws a bit. Lift its leg against the side, at least once. Add a little flavor. Then lap up the filthy water with its big pink tongue. A dog would emerge from the ditch slathering, covered with leeches and some of its own urine, but with its thirst quenched.

Well, he wasn't a dog. He hadn't stooped that low. Not yet.

Without knowing exactly what he was doing Kurt Verfurth found himself walking around the bog a second time. By the time he reached the entrance to the dirt track that would, were he to follow it, take him home he had grown tired. Dog tired. (The irony of that phrase was not lost upon him.) Despite his raging thirst he let himself go limp like a rag next to the bog onto the dry sod that was routinely mown by the crew who, despite the vile rumors about their boss spread by evil tongues, had remained loyal all these years. (He paid them well, too. Kurt Verfurth the dope runner had always understood that loyalty came at a cost.)

Unmindful of his parched throat, oblivious to the merciless sun, he sprawled on the stubby grass and promptly fell asleep.

How long it was that he slept he never knew. Nor precisely what it was that wakened him. The bile that churned in the pit of his stomach? The spider that crawled along the bridge of his nose? His own sonorous snoring? Or the object that, between him and the sun, cast a shadow onto his face?

While he slept that same sun, with its cancer-inducing rays, had badly burned him, had blistered his skin. In one or two spots he may have suffered first-degree burns.

It didn't matter, though. Not in the least. His eyes fluttered open at the same time that a rock the size of a small cantaloupe descended upon them, smashing them, his nose, and his teeth, all at the same time.

CHAPTER XXVII
Dear Diary:

Dear Diary:

Never till this moment have I appreciated the wisdom of the proverb, "Act in haste, repent at leisure." But I have never been wise, have I? How's that other saying go? "Luck is preparation meeting opportunity." Poor Kurt; he wasn't prepared, not at all. Any luck he had, just ran out. Mine, too, I think.

Why did I kill him? Why? It makes no sense. None at all. It's true that I hated him. The lousy kraut. "Love me, love my dog," the saying goes. "Kill me, kill my husband," Amanda might say. (Am I going mad?) And then the sight of him lying there in a drunken stupor…

Now what?

Oh, I know, I know.

I know, only too well.

CHAPTER XXVIII
And Yet Another Wrinkle

One morning in mid August Detective Armenian phoned Lena to say that he would be dropping by that afternoon. He had a number of reasons for wanting to see her, besides asking a few questions; foremost was the hope that she would offer him a piece of her wild blueberry pie.

When he arrived at her door shortly after two he was greeted by the aroma of something baking in the oven. Surely not...?

"You seemed to enjoy my blueberry pie the last time you were here, so I popped one in the oven after you phoned," Lena said, as she ushered him into the library. "I took it out not five minutes ago. Would you care for a piece, once it's had a chance to cool?"

"Well," the detective said, hesitating out of politeness, "since you went to all that trouble and expense..."

"Oh, it was no trouble at all. I love to bake. As for expense, the blueberries are free, there for the picking." She indicated an easy chair. As he sank into it she asked: "Would you like coffee with your pie?"

She went into the kitchen, to return moments later with a tray on which rode two thick slabs of blueberry pie, two cups with saucers, napkins and utensils, a pitcher of cream (no sugar; she'd remembered that he'd declined it for his iced coffee in the gazebo), and a pot of steaming coffee, which she had brewed beforehand. She set the tray on a low table between them, poured them each a cup of coffee, and slid the biggest piece of pie toward her guest.

"You look much better without your war paint," she remarked.

"My war...oh, you mean the calamine lotion." He laughed. "The rash finally cleared up, after a week of misery. No doubt your excellent pie hastened the healing."

Lena gave the detective an opportunity to wolf down the greater portion of his pie before saying: "On the phone you mentioned a few questions."

He nodded, wiped his lips with a paper napkin, and said, "I do have a couple of questions. But my real reason for coming"—other than to partake of blueberry pie—"was to impart information. I feel I can trust you, Mrs. Lombardi. Don't ask me why, but somehow I feel that you may be able to help solve this case."

"So I'm no longer a suspect?"

He smiled. "You never were, not really. Well, I did have my doubts when you insisted we dredge the pond, and especially when you came up with the body yourself."

"It was Pearl Starbuck who found poor Eric, with the help of Old Corpsey."

"Is that what she calls the turtle?"

"It's short for Old Corpse Finder," Lena said.

"At first I thought Officer Mills was pulling my leg when she told me about the snapper. I only wish I could have been there."

"The next time you need help locating a body in water just let me know. I'm sure Miss Starbuck will gladly offer her assistance."

"Speaking of locating bodies...that brings up the subject of why I'm here."

"Oh...?"

"I know I can rely on your discretion, Mrs. Lombardi. The pie was excellent by the way. Top notch."

"Another piece?"

"If you insist."

"I'll be back in a jiffy."

And Lena was back, in less than a jiffy, with the remainder of the pie, eager to hear what he had to say.

"You were about to mention your purpose for being here," she reminded him as he polished off his pie—this second piece larger even than the first.

"A couple of reasons, actually."

He eyed the sole surviving piece, still in the glass baking dish, a wedge-shaped island floating in a pool of purple goo. No no no, he decided; even gluttony must have its limits. Out of pride, if for no other reason, he would forgo the last sliver. And then, too, there was this consolation: if this case should stretch unsolved into the fall harvest season, cranberry pie, made from Mrs. Lombardi's own freshly picked berries, almost certainly would be forthcoming.

"The day of the killings—the day you found Mr. Siminski's body and the day, according to his mother, Mr. Russell went missing—you're quite positive that no one besides the victims drove onto your property? I know we've gone over this before, but I want to make sure we haven't overlooked any possibility. You would have at least heard, if not seen, any other vehicles?"

She nodded. "The only access to the bog by road is through the driveway that goes by this house. The only time I wouldn't hear someone passing by is in the morning when I take my shower. A vehicle might go by unnoticed at that time. But then, I would certainly hear it as it left. I'm not a teenager," she said, jokingly. "I take very quick showers—so as to conserve water. I have an artesian well," she added by way of explanation.

"Isn't there a small river that runs through your property?"

"Oh, but I wouldn't want to drink from that."

He studied her expression to see whether she was pulling his leg. Deciding that she was, he said: "Could anyone have come in on it by boat or canoe?"

She thought for a moment. "I don't think so. In fact, I'm sure they couldn't. At this time of year the water level is low, the banks are steep, and there are too many rapids in either direction. I suppose two people could do it, if they were willing to carry the canoe a good part of the distance." She shook her head. "No. In the long run it would be a lot easier to cross the swamp on foot."

"So whoever killed the two men must have come in by foot. Unless of course he, she, or they—I don't want to make any assumptions here—rode in with them, inside the van."

"I never thought of that possibility," Lena said. "Someone could have been hiding in the back of the van."

"Or have ridden with them by invitation."

"Someone they knew? Like Jay O'Sullivan."

"It's entirely possible," the detective said.

"Or the killer could have parked elsewhere, on one of the side roads that wind through this area, and walked in," Lena said. "Or on one of the properties next to mine. The old Eldredge estate, for instance."

"We've questioned the people who are renting the house; they didn't see anything. But that doesn't mean much." He probed his teeth with the tip of his tongue to dislodge bits of blueberry caught between them, and to ponder. Finally he said: "When you say 'walked in,' how do you mean? Are there trails?"

"Not what you'd call hiking trails," Lena said. "There are any number of old footpaths, for the most part overgrown from disuse, and most of them leading essentially nowhere. And of course animal trails leading to water." She favored him with a smile. "You've had a taste of what it's like."

"It would be easy to get lost in that swamp," Detective Armenian mused. "So it had to have been someone familiar with the area."

"Someone familiar enough to maneuver through swamps," Lena said. "Someone used to the bogs and the terrain that surrounds them. Someone like Harvey Cardozo."

"Who lives on the other side of town," the detective said. "But who could have parked nearby and walked in."

"Or walked clear across. It's not that many miles, as the crow flies. They're rough miles. And there are rivers and streams…But nothing I couldn't have undertaken twenty or thirty years ago. Maybe even now, if my reason for doing so was urgent enough."

"Like murder, you mean?"

She nodded.

"Hmm."

"That's not a confession."

He laughed. "I wasn't thinking of that. I was thinking of the other reason why I wanted to see you."

"Which is…?"

"Mrs. Lombardi, I'm being, uh, unprofessional, that is to say, I'm taking a slight risk in telling you this. But in view of the invaluable assistance you've provided so far"—*not to mention the blueberry pie*, Lena thought—"I think it only fair to keep you up to date."

"I appreciate that," Lena said. "Do have that last piece."

"Oh, but my waistline," Detective Armenian protested, giving his midriff a rueful pat.

"Bosh! It's such a tiny piece. Besides, think of it as fruit, not pie. Here." She snatched his plate and slid the pie onto it, and patiently waited until he had savored the last morsel.

He sighed, from contentment, and the guilt brought on by excess. He would eat lightly that evening, hardly anything, just a small salad, and he would start a diet tomorrow.

"Kurt Verfurth is missing," he said. He leaned forward in his chair, the better, perhaps, to assess Lena's reaction to the news.

"Ah!" Lena exclaimed. "Yet another wrinkle. Did he do a bunk?"

"Pardon me? I don't…"

"Do a bunk. It's underworld slang for 'leave in a hurry.'"

The detective shook his head. "No. That's the strange part. It doesn't look like he did. Three days ago I called him in for questioning, just to go over his testimony."

"To give him the third degree," Lena piped in enthusiastically. "To make him crack."

"He never answered the phone; my calls kept going to his machine. Finally I decided to pay him a visit. The long and short of it is, I found the doors to his house unlocked, his vehicles—his car, the pickup he uses around the bog—parked where he apparently always keeps them. I obtained a warrant, Officer Mills and I searched the house, and—" He shrugged. "It gave all the appearances of someone having stepped out the door with the intention of returning within five or ten minutes."

"Not of someone having flown the coop," Lena chorused. "Even if he did do a bunk, it would not prove his guilt, merely that he was afraid of being arrested. There's no trace of him anywhere?"

"We're searching the property now," Detective Armenian said.

"I'll get on the phone and contact Miss Starbuck." Lena rose form her seat as she spoke.

Armenian held out a hand to restrain her. "Thanks, but right now we're using dogs. If we require the assistance of your friend and her corpse-sniffing turtle I'll let you know." Mindful of future culinary treats, he hastily added: "I do appreciate the offer."

CHAPTER XXIX
Lena Plans a Visit

"Lena! You're gesticulating wildly," Cheryl complained.

"Whatever do you mean?" Lena asked, though it was apparent from her tone of voice that she was not fully focused on what her friend was saying.

"You've been waving your hand about as you talk," Cheryl informed her. "You're acting more fidgety than a hiker who has stumbled into a nest of hornets. You'll be knocking over vases if you're not careful."

"Now dear, it's just my mannerism," Lena said. "Many people talk with their hands. It makes what they say more expressive."

"It's upsetting Marmalade—and me as well. I liked you better when you drank. At least wine calmed you down somewhat."

"Be thankful my hand is not the Beast with Five Fingers," Lena countered.

"The what?"

"The Beast with Five Fingers. I'm alluding to the horror story of that title, about a severed hand which has a will of its own. In the 1940s it was made into a motion picture starring Peter Lorre. At least my hand won't creep up during the night while you're sleeping and throttle you."

"Won't it?" Cheryl glowered at her friend through narrowed eyes but said nothing further.

As an act of contrition Lena lowered her hands to her lap, where she clasped them together and held them tight, is if they were two antagonists locked in mortal combat. "I'll be drinking wine again soon, dear. Once I've avenged those two boys. I made a promise to myself to lay off the stuff until I know for sure who killed them. And right now I think I have a pretty good idea who did."

They were seated in the library, to which they often retired after supper to read and to talk. Marmalade lay on his side in a corner near the hearth, stretched out at full length, head slightly raised, eyes wide open, and sporadically switching his tail—a sure sign of feline perturbation.

"Pure speculation on your part," Cheryl said. "You have absolutely no evidence, concrete or circumstantial. None whatsoever."

"I have intuitive evidence."

"There's no such thing."

Before Lena could contradict her the phone rang. Cheryl, thinking it might be Anthony, went into the kitchen to answer it. "Lena, it's for you," she sang out. "Do you want it in there?"

"I have no secrets to hide from you, dear. Here is fine."

No secrets, just a few dead bodies buried here and there, Cheryl muttered half aloud. Returning to the library she handed over the cordless phone.

It was Detective Armenian. He didn't identify himself (was she fated never to learn the man's actual name?) but Lena recognized his voice.

"Mrs. Lombardi, I have news for you, on the q. t. of course."

"I'm discretion itself," Lena assured him.

"We've located Kurt Verfurth, or rather, his body."

So she was right! "Murdered, like the others?"

"Yeah. It looks like the same m. o. Head bashed in."

"I'm not surprised," Lena said.

"One thing, though. If this is the same perp"—'m. o.' 'perp;' he was beginning to sound just like her—"there's a disturbing pattern. Not that the crimes aren't disturbing enough. But if it is the same individual, he's getting increasingly violent. Verfurth's head was beat to a pulp."

☞☜

174

"This clinches it," Lena declared later that same evening as the two women sat discussing the orgy of violence that continued to impinge upon their lives. The "discretion itself" she had promised Detective Armenian did not preclude confiding in Cheryl of course, whom Lena had sworn to secrecy. "Kurt Verfurth's murder, I mean."

"It exonerates him, that's for sure," Cheryl said. Then after reflection: "Though not necessarily; there's always the possibility that it was he who killed Amanda, and his own murder was a revenge killing, from her lover."

Lena shook her head. "Too complicated a scenario," she said. "And too late in the day. We can apply Ockham's razor and eliminate that theory." Closing her eyes she reclined against the chair but continued to speak, like a medium in rapt communication with the spirit world. "I have a plan," she announced.

The more Cheryl listened to it, the more opposed she became to her friend's harebrained scheme. Though she did not share Lena's certainty of Harvey Cardozo's guilt, she did not have absolute confidence in his innocence, either. He might, or might not, be the killer. The same was true for any number of other suspects. Jay O'Sullivan for instance, or…who else? No one, really. So maybe Harvey did kill Amanda and the others.

If so, he would not hesitate to kill Lena, too.

"I'll be perfectly safe, dear. I won't turn my back on him, and I'll have my .22 pistol with me, fully loaded. You know what a crack shot I am."

The following day Lena initiated her plan with a phone call. The call was intended for Elizabeth Walderne. However it was Elizabeth's "kid sister," Marguerite, who answered.

"Elizabeth is lying down," Marguerite informed her. "We just found out that our neighbor has been murdered. The news upset my sister so much that she became ill."

"Not seriously so, I hope," Lena said—visualizing the overwrought, and overweight, Elizabeth keeling over, like a rhino in full stride felled by a bullet, from stroke or heart attack.

"Just nerves, I believe," Marguerite replied. "The police have been questioning us—as a matter of routine—and the stress has made her sick to her stomach."

"It must be dreadful," Lena sympathized. "knowing that a fiend is stalking the neighborhood."

"Fiend? Whatever do you mean? Surely you don't think we're in any danger?"

"Why, I'm sure you have nothing to fear," Lena reassured her. "So long as you keep your doors locked and remain vigilant. Of course, who am I to talk? I'm nearly as isolated as you—and the killer has already struck here, not just once, but twice." She paused. "It's because of this unpleasant business that I wished to speak with Elizabeth. In fact I thought I might drop by. Incidentally, is your brother-in-law at home?"

"Harvey's in the workshop tinkering with the jalopy in preparation for this fall's harvest. He had intended to repair a dike on one of our bogs, but Elizabeth and I persuaded him not to. You know, because of what happened to Kurt—our neighbor." She hesitated. "Why, did you wish to speak to him as well?"

Lena paused, hoping that Marguerite would interpret her hesitation as reluctance to answer the question. Finally she said: "Actually, it's Harvey I wish to speak to. In person. It's quite important. It's about something that Brian Siminski said to me, shortly before he was murdered."

"In connection to—what's been happening?" Marguerite asked.

"It's nothing I can discuss over the phone," Lena explained. "It has to be in person."

"I see," Marguerite said—sounding, however, far more puzzled than comprehending. "Now is not a good time. My sister as I said is greatly distraught. And I'm a little shaky myself." She gave what sounded like a nervous laugh. "Something so horrible happening so near to us, to a neighbor. The significance hasn't fully sunk in yet—it could have happened to one of us instead of to him." She paused. "Could you come over this evening? Say around seven? I'm sure by then we will have pulled ourselves together. Oh, and you can meet Hooligan."

"Hooligan?"

"Our new Lab. You know, Pal's replacement."

Cheryl was off spending the day with Anthony. At one of the Connecticut casinos. Foxwood? Or was it Mohegan Sun? No matter. Cheryl would not return until late, might even decide to spend the night in Connecticut. It was just as well, her absence. She was a worrywart. She would not approve of, in fact would vigorously oppose, Lena's little stratagem.

Speaking of which: There was one minor detail to attend to. How to conceal the .22 pistol? In the pocket of a lightweight jacket? Although it promised to be a balmy August evening, fall was only a few weeks away. With New England weather one never knew. The night could easily turn chilly; a jacket would not be too conspicuous. She could drape it over one arm, joke about old bones being prepared for any eventuality.

The only thing remaining now was to get through the intervening hours.

At six thirty-five she left the house. All day long Marmalade, sensing her restiveness, had kept close by, rubbing against her calves as if to persuade her to give up her machinations, and like a sensible septuagenarian spend the evening at home with him. She gently nudged him aside with her foot as, jacket in hand, she slipped through the door. As she walked down the portico steps she glanced back. He had positioned himself on the windowsill, like an orange sphinx, unblinking, awaiting her return.

Should she take the car or the pickup? The pickup of course. The drive into the Waldernes' might prove bumpy. Though perhaps not nearly so bumpy as what she had in mind for Harvey.

Or he for her.

CHAPTER XXX
Creatures of the Night

At seven o'clock sharp, Lena turned from the winding back road she had been following for the past five minutes onto the wooded track which, she hoped, led directly to the Waldernes' house. There had been other dirt tracks leading off the frost-heaved tarmac but those presumably led only to bogs, or more precisely, to the network of narrow dirt tracks connecting the various sections of cranberry bog belonging either to the Waldernes (cum Cardozo; she mustn't forget Harvey!) or, now, to the heirs of the late Kurt Verfurth.

The track she selected differed from all the others by having a mail box mounted on a post at its entrance, with the name Walderne hand-painted in faded, black letters. (Evidently when Handsome Harvey married into the family no one had seen fit to add Cardozo to the lettering.) She hadn't passed Kurt Verfurth's mail box. The dirt drive to his house must lie somewhere beyond, well after her turn.

The road in wasn't bumpy after all, or even rutted. The Waldernes kept it well graded with gravel and crushed stone. She followed it, as it twisted and turned—it had probably once been a cart path—for several hundred yards through a mixed-growth forest until she came upon a clearing and beyond the clearing, against a backdrop of bog and swamp, a house and a grouping of outbuildings. The house, a saltbox, looked to be about a hundred years old, its clapboards and cedar shingles weathered to the patina of old silver. It was a large dwelling, built to accommodate a large family, in the days when such families were the rule rather than the exception.

178

No matter. Unless there were distant relatives in line to inherit, this present generation of Waldernes, female and barren, would be the last.

A lawn, of sorts, fronted the house, the pale green of its mangy turf marred by splotches of fecal brown, indicative of a deficiency of fertilizer, lime, and water, a neglect due in all likelihood to indifference rather than sloth. No attempt had been made to landscape the property. The lawn, such as it was, melded into a rough field that bordered the bog and, in places, the swamp. Forsythias, lilac bushes, a few azaleas, a herbaceous border of spent summer blossoms, constituted the ornamental plantings. A vegetable garden, fenced-in (to keep out rabbits and deer, or perhaps Hooligan?), completed the horticultural embellishments.

The outbuildings, a half dozen or so, were in various stages of preservation, some newly repaired (by Brian and Eric? was that the job for which Harvey had hired them?), others about to collapse from decay. Like many old-time cranberry growers, the Waldernes appeared to be land poor, with vast holdings in acreage but little in liquid assets. In a good harvest year they would prosper, buy new equipment, pay off loans, splurge a little; a poor crop, or a low per-barrel price for cranberries (or worse, the two combined), would mean a belt-tightening until next season, or the one after that.

Vehicles were parked on either side of the house: a pickup, a tractor, a bog buggy—presumably the jalopy Harvey had been tinkering with; evidently he had taken it out for a spin—and a rack truck. The SUV was nowhere to be seen. Garaged, probably, in one of the outbuildings. Lena pulled up next to the truck, got out, and went around to the front door, carrying her jacket over her left arm—careful not to let the bulge in one of the pockets show, nor the object within to tumble onto the ground. The flagstones leading to the house were level with the ground, the grass around them neatly trimmed; the Waldernes, if indifferent to appearances, were nevertheless conscientious of safety—all but one of them, perhaps.

With trepidation—her queasiness, she told herself, perfectly understandable under the circumstances—she lifted the brass knocker and rapped it against the door. She stood listening, like a casual visitor uncertain of her welcome, hearing only faint echoes, hollow against the ambient insect buzz of this sultry August evening.

No one came to the door in response to her knock. She allowed a reasonable interval then rapped again, this time more firmly, the raps sharp, like rifle reports. Again no one came. Where were they? In front of a television set, unable to hear? That hardly seemed likely; she was, after all, expected. And where was Hooligan? Should he not by now be barking furiously at the ruckus she was making, audible, surely, to his canine ears?

"Yoohoo," she hollered, in rural just-folks fashion. "Yoohoo!"

Except for the insect buzz, which continued unabated, her hallooing was greeted by silence. Haunted houses must be like this, she thought: the palpable silence, the prickly sensation of someone, some *thing*, listening. She tried the door. Many people residing in the country still, foolishly, left theirs unlocked during daylight hours, some even did so at night; the Waldernes were not among them.

She went around to the rear—as a matter of course, not because she anticipated the likelihood of success. The back steps, leading up to a small deck of pressure-treated planks, were rickety but not unsafe. A dog's dish and bowl were evident, as were a soiled mop, a broom with most of its bristles worn or missing, and a plastic recycling bin overflowing with household refuse. She was tempted to paw through the latter—not in search of clues (how absurd!) but out of curiosity as to how the Waldernes lived. Snooping, in other words.

Resisting the lure of the bin she rapped her knuckles against the frame of the aluminum storm door, at the same time testing the latch; it, too, was locked. Shading her eyes with her palm she peered in, to an empty kitchen. The appliances—refrigerator, stove—seemed fairly new; otherwise the decor looked original to the house: linoleum, bare in spots; tin ceiling; chintz curtains, once brightly colored, now faded to pastels; cast iron sink; enameled metal table; wooden chairs much painted, presently a mustard yellow. The Waldernes, clearly, were not house-proud. Swamp Yankees to the core.

Dirty dishes stacked in the sink gave evidence of a recent meal.

So, where were they? Putting off the dishes for later and taking the dog out for a romp through the woods?

Somehow she couldn't picture that unholy trinity—Harvey, handsome as ever, yet with telltale signs of encroaching age (and blemishes brought on by incipient mania?); Elizabeth, obese, easily winded, flatulent—farting on the sly—chafing between her legs (as many fat people do) from the friction of flab against flab; Marguerite, dour, reticent, self-loathing, if not downright ugly, then plain as sin—she couldn't picture the Walderne-Cardozo threesome out for an evening stroll, drenched in insect repellent, perspiring profusely, idly chatting (what *do* they talk about when together?), or grimly focused, not on one another but on the walk, or in the case of one of them at least, on other, more ominous matters; all the while Hooligan prancing about, splashing through the scum of stagnant ditches, dashing into the swamp after phantom rabbits, gathering unto himself bloodsucking parasites, woodticks and deer ticks—pinhead-size mites which, those that did not adhere to the Lab for their sustenance, would nonetheless hitch a ride into the house, there to crawl loose on carpet, pillow and bedspread, awaiting a more succulent host: the oleaginous Elizabeth.

No, she could not easily picture the three of them out for a walk. Not when she was expected. Not when one of the three, if her hypothesis was correct (and why should it not be?), suspected—feared?—that she, because of broad hints that she had dropped, doubts that she had planted, might be onto something.

Then where in blazes were they?

All sorts of wild imaginings flitted, like rabid bats, through her mind. Harvey, driven over the edge by guilt and fear of discovery, had gone berserk and in a psychotic fury had butchered his wife and sister-in-law before taking his own life. Or worse, having dispatched them (and Hooligan as well), he was at this very moment crouching inside, a mad but wily beast, waiting for her to blunder in so that he might spring from behind sofa or chair and bash in her head with a blunt instrument, the way he had done the others.

Or—and this, though at the expense of injured pride, she had to admit to herself—perhaps she was just a meddling old fool after all and the murderer was not Harvey but someone else entirely, and no one was there to greet her because Marguerite, not appreciating the import of her hints, had neglected to convey her message. Or worse, she may have dismissed Lena as simply a crank, a pest who would probably not show up at all and if she did show up, finding no one at home would eventually go away.

Which is what she was doing now: descending the steps, preparing to leave. It would be getting dark soon; already the air was crepuscular, a diminution of both temperature and light. Before long birds would go to roost and bats emerge from cracks and crevices. This was no place for her to be at night, no place to attempt to trap a supposed murderer—on his home ground. Next time—if there was a next time—she would choose her moment, and her playing field, more wisely.

She had nearly traversed the length of the lawn to her pickup, when she heard distant shouting: someone, a woman's voice, calling out her name. The shouts came from a clearing on the far side of a section of bog from which a dirt road led into the swamp. A woman emerged from the swamp running, calling out her name, at the same time waving frantically with both arms, a semaphore of flailing limbs, as if sound alone or waving just one arm might fail to capture Lena's attention.

Despite distance and the fading light Lena recognized the woman as Marguerite Walderne. What possessed the poor fool? She acted like a castaway on a desert island who has at long last spotted the sails of a passing vessel. Could Lena's being just a few minutes late for an agreed upon meeting warrant such frenetic behavior? Surely something must be seriously wrong.

Maintaining a secure grip on the jacket, the bulge in its pocket prevented from slipping loose by her tightened fingers, Lena waved with her free hand to signal that she was aware of Marguerite's approach; she began to walk toward the running figure, taking her time, anxious to hurry but not wishing to come to grief on the uneven turf.

Almost as soon as she had started she halted, having remembered that in a short while there would be very little light by which to see. With an about-face she returned to her pickup and removed a flashlight from behind the seat. It was the same flashlight she used on frost nights when, not trusting the growers' service to be one hundred percent diligent, she went around her bog in the wee hours checking for clogged sprinkler heads. She tested the battery. It was strong and cast a bright, dependable beam.

So as not to be encumbered, in defiance of the August heat she slipped on the jacket before resuming her walk. By now Marguerite had covered half the distance that separated them. Obviously winded, she no longer ran but instead lurched forward, as if willing herself in spurts. As they converged Lena could see that the woman was near exhaustion, her face red from exertion, her clothing—tan top, khaki shorts—drenched in sweat.

"Mrs. Lombardi…" she gasped, panting, when finally they were close enough to converse without having to shout.

"What is it, Miss Walderne? Has something happened?"

Marguerite buried her face in her hands, her frame wracked with sobs, but after a short while she pulled herself together and taking a deep breath blurted out: "There's been another…I found…oh I can't believe this is happening." She gazed frantically into Lena's eyes, as if she sought sanctuary there. "I think he's dead but I'm not sure. I know I should have stayed with him but…"

"Someone's hurt? Badly?"

Marguerite nodded. "His head…oh God, his head!"

"We've got to call for help," Lena said, and turned toward the house.

"I called 9-1-1 on my cell phone," Marguerite said. "They're sending an ambulance and cruisers." Trembling, she removed a soiled handkerchief from her pocket and wiped the grime from her face. "I should have stayed with him but I just couldn't bear to. Besides," she added, with a sweep of her hand indicating the half dozen dirt tracks leading off in all directions, "how would they ever find us out there? They wouldn't know which way to take."

"If he's still alive we can't just leave him alone, at the mercy of…whatever," Lena said, thinking, not without a shudder, of the vultures that had clustered around Pal. There would be no vultures abroad at this hour, of course. But there would be other scavengers, and predators, creatures of the night who might not be too particular

183

as to whether their intended meal was actually dead or just barely breathing. "Not if there's a chance he may pull through. I don't know what we can do but there must be *something*." She looked uncertainly in the direction of her pickup, weighing the pros and cons of setting off in it in aid of…what? A dead or dying man? "Can you tell me what happened? And who is it that's hurt? Not your brother-in-law?"

Marguerite shook her head. "It's not Harvey thank God." She raised her hands in a gesture of helplessness. "I don't know what happened, Mrs. Lombardi. Well, of course I do. The person that killed Kurt Verfurth has struck again. What other explanation can there be?"

"But who's this new victim?" Lena wondered aloud.

"I think," Marguerite began, then faltered. "I think it's a man named Jay O'Sullivan. I'm not sure because his face is…How can a person do that to another human being?"

"We've got to act," Lena said. "But how?"

"I think he's beyond help, Mrs. Lombardi. Far beyond any help we can give." Cocking her head in the posture of someone straining to hear, she said: "We should be hearing sirens soon. In the meantime I'm frightened. He's still out here."

It took only a second or two for Lena to comprehend the significance of that "he." Yes, *he* was still out here. And it was rapidly growing dark.

"We'd best go into the house," she said. "And keep the doors locked until the police arrive."

With Marguerite in the lead, they moved quickly toward the house. Lena was glad for the flashlight; even assisted by its beam they had to walk cautiously in the coarsening twilight, to avoid rough spots. Marguerite made a beeline for the back door. With what, under different circumstances, might have been amusement Lena watched as Marguerite, kneeling, reached over the side of the deck to retrieve a house key attached by a magnet to the underside. So typical of country folk, to hide a key in the first place a burglar would look!

Marguerite pushed through the doorway into the kitchen, waited for Lena to follow, then switched on the overhead light and with trembling fingers locked the door behind her. The air inside the house was stifling, causing Lena to remove her jacket. Marguerite, red as a beet (there was something about the woman that called up clichés), mopped at her brow again. They stood awkwardly for a moment or two, as if seeking direction from one another, until taking the initiative Lena drew a chair away from the table and sat, keeping the jacket humped in her lap like a sleeping cat. She set the flashlight bulb-end down on the linoleum beside her. Marguerite continued to stand.

She did not remain still for long, instead began to pace nervously, glancing every few seconds it seemed at the clock on the wall. The clock was of black acrylic, in the shape of a teapot, a novelty, if memory served Lena correctly, which had been popular back in the forties or fifties. Lena's parents had owned such a clock, only theirs had been red. What had happened to it? she wondered.

She took note of the time: five past eight.

Harvey and Elizabeth—where were they? In the excitement she had forgotten them entirely.

"Where are your sister and brother-in-law?" she asked.

"Visiting Harvey's cousin in Mansfield. He's a dog lover, too; they're showing off Hooligan." She paused. "I don't expect them back until late."

Is that what he told you? Lena thought. You poor deluded fool. Harvey isn't in Mansfield. He's out there, right now, lurking, on the prowl, waiting for night to fall—after having done Lord knows what with, or to, your sister. Poor Elizabeth. Poor cow.

Jay O'Sullivan his latest victim! That would lend credence to Lena's own theory, clinch it really, that the boys saw something on that fateful night ten years ago when Amanda Verfurth was murdered. Now they—all five of them—were dead, too. There were no more witnesses.

She, however, remained. If Harvey, through Marguerite, had taken the hint, that she knew something, that Brian had confided in her…But if he had taken it, why had he chosen not to meet with her this evening?

Jay O'Sullivan—had he thrown the proverbial monkey wrench into the gears? Had he shown up unexpectedly—for purposes of blackmail?—forcing Harvey to change whatever carefully worked-out plans he may have had for dealing with Lena? Had Marguerite even told Harvey about their telephone conversation?

She was about to query Marguerite on the subject when the latter abruptly stopped pacing and throwing her hands into the air in a gesture of anguish exclaimed: "I can't take this any longer. Someone should have been here by now. We're not that remote from town!"

"When you made that call on your cell phone," Lena said, "you must have been overwrought, perhaps in shock. Are you sure you conveyed sufficient information? I don't know how these things work, but if you were out there"—she gestured vaguely toward the swamp—"maybe they couldn't pick up your exact coordinates, if that's the right term."

Marguerite sighed. "I thought I made myself clear but maybe you're right. I'll call again, this time on the land phone. It's in the living room. I'll be right back." Still dabbing at her forehead with the handkerchief, she crossed the kitchen into the adjoining room.

Did she intend to make the call in the dark? Lena wondered, noticing, now that the sun had sunk behind the trees, how densely dark the night had become. The window panes showed solid black, like sheets of coal. There seemed to be no moon, no stars. Had there been a cloud cover earlier? She couldn't remember. Her mind had been on other things.

A high-pitched scream pierced her train of thought. The scream came from the next room. Marguerite!

She shot up from the chair. Unmindful of the jacket in her lap, she let it slide to the floor where it landed with a muffled *clunk*. Damn! She bent over and fumbled for the gun. In the two seconds it took her to extricate it from the pocket in which it had become entangled, the cruel realization raced through her mind: Harvey! In the house all this time!

Gun in hand, and hardly aware of the stiffness in her joints, or the fact that her left leg had fallen asleep, she half limped, half ran toward the living room. It was the limp that in the end saved her. By slowing her down it gave her precious seconds to think, to collect her thoughts, so that at the threshold she paused. Why were there no more screams, no more sounds? Had Harvey clasped a hand over his sister-in-law's mouth? Was he even now bending back her head to snap her spine? Had Marguerite fainted?

As Lena lunged across the threshold into darkness she had no further time for thought, no time to work out the details of what the scream, and the subsequent silence, might signify. No time to grabble for a light switch.

Before her was an uncharted sea. As she took the time to grope through shoals of unknown objects a formless blur loomed from the murk, an inchoate mass that quickly took shape as it lunged toward her: Marguerite, a crowbar in her upraised hand.

Lena froze. At the last moment she dodged to one side, twisted her body around and aimed the gun—to wound, not to kill—and squeezed the trigger. Her aim was off. The bullet struck her assailant full in the chest, not in the intended arm. Marguerite, her momentum stalled by the impact, fell dead onto the floor, the crowbar crashing down beside her.

Stunned, Lena stood in the shadows looking down at the felled woman. After what seemed a long time but was probably only a minute or two she stepped back from the living room into the kitchen, into the light, and stared at the gun in her hand with dismay.

She was not such a crack shot after all.

EPILOGUE

All Sorted Out

"Detective Armenian has it all sorted out, dear. It seems that Marguerite kept a diary. Can you imagine!"

The two women, Lena Lombardi and Cheryl Fernandes, were—as was their custom after supper—seated in the library. On a scatter rug between them lay Lena's cherished orange tabby, Marmalade, stretched out at full length like an overripe butternut squash. Lena had, many years ago, when her fingers were nimble, braided the rug on which he reposed from strips of woolen cloth torn from discarded winter coats purchased at rummage sales; its subdued colors, gray, brown, tan, maroon, befitted the women's present somber mood.

Though shared by both, the mood seemed destined to remain somber, or sober, for not very long. For between them, next to and towering over the cat, reposed a sommelier's cart, on which were laid out all the accouterments requisite for an evening of quiet celebration: Waterford crystal, ice bucket, wine towels, and two bottles of a not over priced though by no means inexpensive Champagne.

"That helped, of course," Lena continued, referring to Marguerite's ill-advised diary. "And Harvey confessed. That helped, too." She inclined her head toward the bucket. "Would you do the honors, dear? The last time I uncorked Champagne it gushed out like a geyser. I lost nearly a full glass of the precious stuff, not to mention the mess it made."

Cheryl lifted the bottle from the bucket. "Harvey confessed? To what? I thought you said Marguerite killed Amanda, as well as the others." She removed the stiff metal foil from the cork, twisted off

189

the protective wire, and with the aid of a linen towel that Lena had neatly folded to one side of the tray, yanked out the cork.

Pop.

"There, not a drop wasted," Cheryl said with a self-congratulatory smile. She poured them each a glass.

"A most gratifying sound," Lena murmured, before addressing her friend's question. "Harvey confessed to having moved Amanda's body and burying it on one of her cranberry bogs, which of course is next to his. Oh, and to having had an affair with her."

She accepted the glass proffered by Cheryl. "A toast," she proposed, raising it. As their crystals clinked she said: "To justice. And to the memory of Brian and Eric, neither of whom deserved to die so young. And I suppose I should include Kurt Verfurth; he was, after all, a victim, albeit an unsavory one. As for Mr. O'Sullivan: *nil nisi bonum*; I have nothing good whatsoever to say about him."

"Two questions," Cheryl said, after her initial sip. "Why did Marguerite kill Amanda? And why did Harvey conceal the body? To protect his sister-in-law? That doesn't seem to add up."

"I'll answer your second question first," Lena said. "Harvey wasn't protecting Marguerite; he was protecting, or thought he was protecting, his wife. Absurd as it sounds, Harvey assumed it was Elizabeth—bovine, cud-chewing Elizabeth—who committed the murder. Out of jealousy. Shortly before finding Amanda dead he thought he saw his wife leaving the scene. And he did see her. But she just happened to be nearby, oblivious to any wrongdoing, walking whatever Pal / Hooligan avatar was current at the time. Once he found out the truth—that she hadn't killed Amanda—it was too late. Burying a murder victim on someone else's property—or even on your own—is a serious offense. Besides, how, having moved and concealed the body, thereby destroying crucial evidence, could he ever prove to the authorities that he was innocent of the more grievous felony, murder?"

She paused for a moment to savor her wine. "But I'm getting ahead of myself. Marguerite's motive? She killed Amanda because— and the evidence for this, according to our detective friend, is in the diary—she was, in her twisted way, madly in love with Harvey.

'Madly' is the operative word here, dear. In a sense Marguerite's to be pitied. Not that she didn't deserve to die for what she did. She deserved far worse than death. She deserved to spend the rest of her life in a prison for the criminally insane. I did her a favor, shooting her in the heart. There's something symbolic about that, don't you agree? Or perhaps I should have shot her in the head. That's where her true sickness resided."

Cheryl stared at her friend, appalled. "Lena! How can you say such things?" She reached over and patted the older woman's hand. "I know, it's your way of coping with—what happened. But you mustn't blame yourself. You didn't intend to kill Marguerite. It all happened so fast; you acted instinctively."

"Pshaw. I don't blame myself, dear." She refilled Cheryl's glass, then her own. "If I do blame myself for anything, it's for getting the whole thing wrong. I had myself convinced that it was Harvey who was going around bashing in heads." She shook her head in disbelief. "Marguerite was such a consummate actress; you should have seen the performance she put on for me. I suppose she'd dissembled all her life, presenting a mask to the world, hiding her true emotions. She should have been in the movies. Of course, given those looks of hers, they would have to have been horror movies."

"If as you say," Cheryl mused, "Marguerite was in love with Harvey, in however a pathological way, why did she stop at killing just his girlfriend? Why not his wife as well? Certainly she didn't refrain from doing away with Elizabeth out of sibling affection?"

"You never got a really good look at Marguerite, did you, dear? Just a glimpse through the window, that time they came in search of their missing Lab. She really was ill-favored, you know. Coarse, plain, one might say reptilian. Now, there are some women who are downright ugly, but who are not entirely unattractive to the opposite sex; they may even exude an aura of sexuality. Marguerite, alas, was not among their number. And she knew it. I've known women as lacking in beauty as she was, who have nonetheless found husbands or lovers and who, apparently, live very happy lives. I don't think Marguerite was capable of happiness. I think she despised herself; who knows what her childhood was like."

"Okay, granted," Cheryl said. "She had no hope of, what's the word, 'winning' Harvey. So what was the point of killing Amanda?"

"To preserve the Walderne-Cardozo *ménage à trois*." Lena held her glass to the light in admiration of the tiny bubbles that percolated to the top. "I sometimes think the flavor is in the bubbles as much as it is in the Champagne," she said.

Cheryl, all too familiar with her friend's artifices, said: "All right, Lena, out with it. Tell me all you know about this '*ménage à trois*.'"

"Oh, very little, dear. It's all speculation. Though Detective Armenian has dropped a few hints…garnered from Marguerite's diary I suppose." She glanced at her glass, and seeing that it was nearly empty said: "Open that second bottle, would you, dear." She smiled knowingly. "Harvey's been rather tight-lipped about the exact relationship the three of them, uh, enjoyed. But then why wouldn't he be? He's still married to Elizabeth.

"I see a number of possibilities," she went on, when Cheryl had performed her vinous duties and replenished their glasses. "Harvey married Elizabeth for financial security; he may be handsome, but he's utterly feckless; he could hardly have succeeded at anything on his own. Marguerite came as part of the dowry. Whether his relationship with her was conventional or something less than platonic we'll likely never know. She may have enjoyed his favors; or it may be that she resigned herself to merely being in proximity to him on a daily basis. Love affects people in strange ways. As does sexual frustration."

Closing one eye, Cheryl squinted at her glass with the other, like a jeweler examining a questionable stone. "Unlike Champagne, which affects people—I, alas, being no exception—in all too familiar ways. I think I like the brut better than the extra dry," she said. "Don't you?" Without waiting for a reply she asked: "What prompted Marguerite to go on a homicidal spree? I think I have an inkling as to why but go ahead and tell me."

"To understand the answer we have to go back to that fatal night ten years ago," Lena said. "I may have been dead wrong about the identity of the killer, but I was right about one thing: Brian and his friends saw something that night. (It's all in Harvey's confession, by

192

the way.) Brian's brother, familiar with the area from having worked on the bogs, suggested it as an ideal spot for their underage drinking. After all, who besides themselves would be out there after dark?

"But Harvey was out there, burying Amanda under the vines. And at some point the boys observed him. Brad of course recognized him. Though inebriated, or perhaps *because* they were inebriated, they approached him and—this was almost certainly Jay O'Sullivan's idea—demanded money in return for their silence: blackmail. He agreed—what else could he do, confronted by four drunken teenagers and their equally drunken but slightly older ringleader?—and promised them money in return for their silence. The payoff was to take place in a day or two."

"But then the boys got into a terrible accident," Cheryl interposed. "That changed everything, I imagine."

"It did indeed," Lena said. "For one thing it delayed the payoff. More important it reduced the number of payees. Brad and the Britto boy were dead; Eric though alive was, because of his brain injuries, no longer of consequence. It was fully three weeks before Jay, a reluctant Brian tagging along, met up with Harvey—who now had a bargaining chip. He had seen the boys driving off that night, with Jay, not Brad as they had claimed, at the wheel.

"The upshot of it is, he gave Jay and Brian each a couple of grand to keep quiet, and at the same time declared that that was it—no more would be forthcoming. By then he knew that, whoever had killed Amanda, it wasn't Elizabeth; in fact, like almost everyone else he now assumed it was her husband who killed her. Jay and Brian could go to the police if they liked; it would be their word against his. The word of two drunken witnesses, not five. He would take his chances, by telling some lie or other—oh, and incidentally, if need be, he would let the police know who was operating their vehicle when it left his property."

She paused to lubricate her vocal cords with two or three quick swallows. "So you preferred the first bottle, the brut?"

"They're both excellent," Cheryl said. "But the brut is a bit dryer. Though it's not a strong preference, brut would be my first choice."

"Ah, we've become such connoisseurs," Lena declared. "I can

remember when I was content with a fifty-cent bottle of muscatel wine."

"That must have been quite some time ago," Cheryl said, laughing.

"It was, dear. When I was a teenager, doing *my* underage drinking."

"So," Cheryl said, "the boys took the money and went their merry way."

"Not exactly merry, dear. Brian, from every indication, was wracked with guilt, first because of his brother's death, second because of his part in the blackmail, and also I think for not coming forth and telling what he had witnessed. Oh, and for what happened to Eric as well. As for Jay O'Sullivan, he was a bad egg from the get-go."

"And then…" Cheryl prodded.

"And then Amanda's bones turned up."

"Prompting…"

"Prompting Marguerite to kill again." Lena glanced at her empty glass, decided that it was better that it remain so for the nonce, and continued. "She may not have intended to actually kill Amanda, merely to scare her off; she may have struck her in anger, then seeing what she had done, fled the scene. But the other murders were premeditated, no doubt about that."

"But why?" Cheryl asked. "Why kill Brian and Eric?"

"To silence them. She knew about the blackmail; Harvey told his wife about it, when he still believed that she had killed Amanda; and Elizabeth confided in her sister. When the remains came to light Jay, figuring that the accident, and his responsibility for causing it, had long been forgotten—the statute of limitations may have run out—renewed his demands on Harvey for money. But Jay wasn't the immediate problem. He could be put off, perhaps with a small payment, and taken care of later. Her immediate concern was Brian.

"She was afraid that if Kurt Verfurth was accused of his wife's murder, as seemed likely, Brian, to save an innocent man, would come forth with what he knew. So she killed him. And Eric for the same reason, or simply because he was in the way. She lured him to the kettle hole, struck him from behind, and weighted his body

194

down with rocks and chains she had prepared ahead of time. You see, she knew the swamps almost as well as I do; what else did she have to do all day, but roam about?"

"But…"

"If you want to know why she killed Kurt, I can't answer that, dear. Out of maniacal impulse? Blood lust? Fear that he might be proved innocent, and then what? Or on the possibility that he had an alibi for the time Eric and Brian were killed, so that if the police linked their killings with Amanda's, he would no longer be the prime suspect?" She shrugged. "According to Detective Armenian, the killings became increasingly violent. After all, she came at me with a crowbar, and all I had done was hint that I might know something."

"That didn't make any sense," Cheryl said. "Trying to kill you."

"Evidently it did to her," Lena replied. "No sense letting the rest of this Champagne go flat." She glanced at Cheryl, who shook her head, then poured the one or two remaining fingers into her own glass. "Marguerite had it all planned, and she might have gotten away with it. Killing both Jay and me, I mean." She sipped her Champagne, smacking her lips as if sampling it for the first time.

"Poor Jay," she mused. "His timing was all off. He was there to collect blackmail, but got something else instead: a bullet between the eyes."

"A bullet?" Cheryl said. "Not head bashed in like the others? If Marguerite had suddenly gone high tech—from blunt objects to a gun—why did she attack you with a crowbar? Wouldn't a gun have been easier—not to mention, given what happened to her in the end, a lot more dependable?"

Lena shook her head. "She wanted to pin the murders on Jay. Had her plan succeeded she would have concocted some story about Jay killing me, and her killing him in self-defense. She did tell the truth about one thing: Harvey and Elizabeth were visiting his cousin in Mansfield." She stared at her empty glass with regret. "The Walderne-Cardozo household has been reduced from a *ménage à trois* to a *folie à deux*—that is, if we leave Hooligan out of the equation." She sighed. "Marguerite is being buried tomorrow. Do you think it would be tacky of me to attend the funeral?

The End